Praise for Jess Dee's *Photo Opportunity*

Rating: Reviewer Choice Award Nominee "Photo Opportunity is one erotic romance you don't want to miss. Packed with emotion, fun and a whole lot of sexual tension, this book grabs your attention literally from the first sentence."

~ *Trang, Ecataromance*

"Photo Opportunity is wonderfully delicious. Jess Dee made me cry and ripped out my heart. She gave me that kind of feeling that you get when something is about to go very wrong and your heart just drops to the pit of your stomach. Talk about a roller coaster ride..."

~ *Jambrea, Joyfully Reviewed*

Rating: Five Angels "If you are looking for a romance with a hero who knows from the start where his heart lays – and is determined to follow it – then I heartily recommend Photo Opportunity to you. This tale will prove to be everything you are looking for."

~ *Elizabeth, Fallen Ang*

Rating: Ten Cupids "PF   dicting read. MS. DEE has done   in her reader and keeping their atte

~ *Marina, Cupid's Library Reviews*

Rating: Five Hearts "I seriously loved this story. To watch Daniel and Amy go around in circles trying to figure out their relationship makes a great read! I recommend it highly!"

~ *Brenda, The Romance Studio*

Rating: Recommended Read "Jess Dee...created a beautiful story of life-long friendships."

~ *Melinda, My Book Cravings*

Look for these titles by
Jess Dee

Now Available:

Ask Adam
A Question of Trust

Circle of Friends Series
Circle of Three: Only Tyler (Book 1)

Coming Soon:

Circle of Friends Series
Circle of Three: Steve's Story (Book 2)

Photo Opportunity

Jess Dee

A Samhain Publishing, Ltd. publication.

Samhain Publishing, Ltd.
577 Mulberry Street, Suite 1520
Macon, GA 31201
www.samhainpublishing.com

Photo Opportunity
Copyright © 2009 by Jess Dee
Print ISBN: 978-1-60504-151-3
Digital ISBN: 1-59998-930-1

Editing by Jennifer Miller
Cover by Scott Carpenter

First Samhain Publishing, Ltd. electronic publication: May 2008
First Samhain Publishing, Ltd. print publication: March 2009

Dedication

With special thanks to Samhain Publishing and my wonderful editors, Jennifer and Carrie, for saving this book.

Chapter One

Daniel Tanner was a man who knew what he wanted, and what he wanted most lay naked on his bed, quivering in the aftermath of her second orgasm. The first two he gave freely. The third she would have to work for.

Her taste lingered in his mouth, a mixture of cream, honey and sex. He resisted the urge to lean down and taste her again. Instead his gaze swept over her body, taking in the swollen breasts, their dusky pink nipples puckered into tight beads. Her chest rose and fell in unison with her long, hard puffs, and her toned, shapely thighs were spread in invitation. The damp cleft between her legs glistened and Daniel thought he might well have a heart attack if he didn't fuck her soon.

He ran a finger over her engorged clit and her hips bucked.

"Daniel…" Her softly voiced gasp was music to his ears.

Her gaze locked with his as he brought his finger to his mouth and licked. Green eyes turned hazy with desire and she moaned out loud.

He raked his fingers lightly over her breasts.

"Daniel, please…" She pushed her chest up, begging for more. He watched as she twisted on the sheets. Color tinged her cheeks and her hair spilled over the pillow in a tangled cloud.

She never looked sexier. Emotion washed through him, so

powerful he shook. He fantasized about this moment forever and could hardly believe it was finally happening.

"Yeah, babe?" He knew what she wanted, but still waited for her to beg.

"Oh..." Frustration flashed across her face, and he couldn't repress his slow, satisfied smile. She was in no state to talk, not after what he'd just done to her. He'd give her another minute. Watching her writhe like that was almost as arousing as watching her come.

"Please," she said again and moaned.

"What do you want?" he whispered.

"You."

"Show me."

She whimpered and twisted again. With a strangled cry, she brought her hands up and cupped her breasts. Her fingers worked desperately at the taut peaks, pinching and kneading until she moaned aloud.

Blood shot to Daniel's cock. A muffled groan caught in his throat and he rasped, "How does that feel?"

"So...good." Her mouth opened the tiniest bit and the tip of her tongue touched her lower lip.

His heart heaved and his body went into overdrive. "Hey, sweetheart..." He drew his finger through her slick folds. She looked at him with pupils so dilated the emerald irises were barely visible. "You want more?"

She gave a vague nod.

"Want my finger?" He dipped it inside, and she jerked against his hand.

She shook her head.

"How about if I kiss you again?" He leaned down and licked her, replacing his finger with his tongue.

10

She shivered.

"No..." Her voice drifted from a million miles away. They both knew what she needed.

"So what is it you want?" He licked her again...and then again because quite frankly, she tasted too good to stop.

"You," she moaned. "I want you."

"How?" She was so wet, so hot. Her juices trickled down his chin.

"Daniel..."

"Tell me how you want me," he said then tongued her again.

Her hands left her breasts. He felt them as they wound through his hair. Felt the mild sting as she tugged, forcing his head up. Felt them as she pulled him into position so he now lay on top of her, his face inches from hers.

Then she moved her hands to his cheeks and held his face still. Their eyes met.

Could she see how he felt? Was the raw emotion gripping his gut visible to her? She knew everything about him. Was it really possible she didn't know he loved her?

Full breasts pressed into his chest, her nipples hard against his bare skin. She shifted her legs an inch so that he slid between her thighs. The tip of his cock brushed her slit and he bit the inside of his cheek, praying the pain would dampen his urgency.

She pulled his face down, opened her lips under his and kissed him. The deep, thorough movement of her mouth inflamed him until he blazed with hunger and need.

He had to have her—possess her—so she could know, once and for all, she was his.

"Tell me what you want, babe." Whatever it was, he'd give it

11

to her.

"You," she said then kissed him again, her mouth warm and intoxicating. "I want you—" she sucked on his lip and then bit it, "—to make love to me."

Exquisite pain shot from his mouth to his groin. He barely had time to register it before she shimmied her hips and raked her fingernails down his back.

"Now," she gasped.

Daniel was pretty sure she drew blood, but he didn't give a damn. The only thing he cared about was burying himself inside her hot, wet core. He edged the tip of his cock in and groaned in pleasure.

"Now, Danny!" There was a frantic quality to her voice. She spread her legs wider and took him in deeper. "Do it."

His restraint fractured. With a skilled, desperate thrust, he filled her.

"Yes!"

Nothing in his life had ever felt this good, this right. This was where he belonged.

Moving slowly, he slid all the way out and then back in again. Twice. Three times. Then out. He stopped. Just to prolong the sweet agony of it all.

She moaned and writhed beneath him. He held himself still, his weight resting on his lower arms. His muscles corded and tensed as he watched her. Sweat beaded on his forehead and behind his shoulders.

"Daniel...please." Her hand snuck between their hips. It pressed against him, circled his dick and then moved on to caress his balls.

He groaned out loud and lost it altogether. Grinding his pelvis into hers, he buried himself so deep in her hot body he had to grit his teeth to stop from coming. Unable to suppress his need for her, he pulled out and plunged into her again and again, in long, deep movements.

She met him thrust for thrust. Her legs wound around his waist. She wrapped her arms around his neck, tilted her pelvis upward and opened herself wider for him.

Gratified, he moved harder, faster, hearing her excited moans.

The feel of her, hot and tight and wet, encasing him in her velvety depths, added to the friction against his rigid cock...it was all too incredible. His body moved of its own accord, faster, faster, harder, harder, until her muscles clamped down violently and she screamed his name, and spasm after spasm rocked her body.

He gave one last, mighty thrust. His balls tightened and his body stilled. Pleasure slammed through him.

"I love you, Amy!" He came, his climax potent as he emptied himself into her shivering depth. Again and again he shuddered as the last drops of come drained from his body.

Finally. He'd finally branded her. She was his. There was no way she was getting away from him now.

Daniel shuddered one last time, collapsed on top of her and woke up.

For several minutes he lay still, panting on his bed—alone.

"God damn it." His fingers curled into frustrated fists and he pounded the bed. "Damn it!"

Shit. It was only Tuesday and he already had the dream twice this week. How much more torture did one man have to endure? Enough already. He wanted the real thing. All this dreaming about fucking her just wasn't good enough anymore.

It was this damn assignment. It was doing his head in.

Making him face issues he wasn't ready to face. Think about things he'd long since suppressed.

A primal growl sounded deep in his throat. The images from the dream still reverberated through his head, leaving him aroused and uncomfortable. Hell, he was hard and hurting. And there was only one thing—one woman—who could take away that pain.

She just didn't know it.

Daniel threw off the sheets and marched into the bathroom, turning on the shower. He adjusted the temperature and pressure until burning streams of water jettisoned over his knotted back and shoulders.

He'd always known, always loved her. At fourteen years of age, Daniel lost his heart forever. He took one look at the beautiful adolescent girl and knew one day in the future they'd be together.

But teenagers just didn't make lifelong commitments. Hell, they could barely cope with month-long commitments. So Daniel decided to do the next best thing: commit to being Amy's lifelong friend. His decision had set the course of their relationship for the next seventeen years. Amy became his best friend, his confidante, his pal. And secretly, his greatest love.

He watched in silence as first boys, then men, dated and wooed her. He stood on the sidelines as she fell in and out of love. As any good friend would, he supported her through break-ups and make-ups, highs and lows. She called him her rock and made him vow he'd always be in her life, always be her closest friend.

Daniel scrubbed his body clean, praying the lingering arousal brought on by the dream would be washed down the drain with the soapy water. He didn't hold much hope. All he need do was think about Amy and he'd be hard again.

Of course he promised her—and he never went back on his word. But now it was time to take their friendship to a new level, to a more meaningful one. The last three months had taught him life was too short to screw around. He learned if he wanted something, he had to go after it, grab it and hold on for dear life. It was time to act on the feelings he developed as a teenager. Only he intended to turn them into very adult actions.

There was just one problem.

Amy didn't return his feelings. Convincing her to fall in love with him was going to be the most difficult—and most important—task Daniel had ever undertaken. He damn well better not fail.

She was too comfortable in their platonic friendship. Too freaked out by men in general to consider him anything more than her best mate. And way too sure he was incapable of commitment.

Up until a couple of months ago she would have been right. Commitment to another woman had never been his thing. He thoroughly enjoyed his bachelor years—in fact, thrived on them. So much so, he put his feelings for Amy aside and got on with his life. Good sex and short flings had fulfilled every desire, every need he had. But now everything was different. Now Amy was the only one he wanted. He just had to prove it to her.

She'd never believe him. The irony was, if she ever got wind of what he thought about her, she'd hightail it out of his life before he had a chance to act. Sure, she loved him...like the proverbial brother. That's all he was to her—her best friend. Which was okay for the time being. Anything more than that would scare the living wits out of her. Since Simon the asshole had cheated on her, she was pissed off at men in general. Not surprising really since Simon's behavior mirrored her father's actions of several years before.

Simon's infidelity had reinforced every tiny bit of insecurity Amy experienced as a child, watching her father first cheat on her mother several times over and then abandon his wife and daughter.

Although terrified of taking a chance, Amy had put her fear of betrayal aside, and poured her soul into loving and trusting Simon. In return he'd left her with nothing but heartache and doubt, just like her father had. Two men, both central and significant figures in her life, had both turned into unfaithful, disloyal bastards.

Daniel gritted his teeth. Christ, he despised Simon. Always had. But he'd put his feelings aside so as not to hurt Amy— who'd seriously loved the asshole. Daniel was not a violent man by nature, but if Amy had not held him back, he would have happily rearranged the turd's face after the incident.

No wonder Amy was terrified of believing in another man. The only reason she spoke to Daniel was because he was just her friend. She didn't judge him, she simply accepted him. Daniel. Her friend. Period.

How could he explain that the last three months had changed him? That memories he'd put aside decades ago, and issues he'd sorted out as a boy, had come careening back, devastating him with their clarity? Would Amy understand that after speaking to one young child, he'd been hit by an epiphany? That the child had made him see life from a very different perspective. She'd helped him choose a very different future from the one he'd been heading towards.

He'd asked himself these questions—repeatedly. Now he knew the answers, he knew what had to be done.

Feeling decidedly less agitated, he switched off the shower, grabbed a towel and dried himself off. He had a plan and it was time to implement it. Daniel walked to the phone and dialed his sister.

Without preamble, he launched straight into conversation when she picked up. "Hey, Lex. Remember that conversation you and I had a few days ago? The one about Amy?"

"Mm-hmm," came Lexi's sleepy response on the other end of the line. "How could I forget?"

"I'm ready to put my plan into action."

"You are?" Her voice was alert now.

"Yes. The question is, are you?"

"I'll need a little time. Can you give me a week?"

"I'll give you two. Maybe we can make it coincide with your birthday?"

Daniel could almost see her nod as she answered. "Good idea."

"Great. Now, one thing. Don't tell Mum. You know her. She'll be arranging a wedding before you've even put the phone down."

"Can I at least tell Sarah?"

Daniel blanched at the thought of her telling their older sister. "Hell no. She'd pack up Ben's old cot and his entire baby wardrobe and deposit them all at my flat by sunset."

Lexi laughed then her tone became serious. "You sure you're ready for this, Danno? We both know your plan could backfire."

A muscle worked in his jaw. He knew well the risk he was taking. If his plan was successful, Amy would be his best friend and lover. If his plan failed, Amy could wind up being neither.

The thought made him sick to his stomach.

"I'm ready for this." It was true. He'd never been more ready for anything in his life.

There was a moment of silence on the line and then Lexi spoke again. "Right...sounds like your mind's made up, so let's stop wasting time. We've a seduction to plan. I don't care how long it takes—I intend to see it through to the end."

Daniel felt the tension in his ribs ease. He even managed to smile. "I appreciate your help, Lex. But if this ends the way I intend it to, you most definitely will not be there to see it."

Lexi snorted. "Can I at least be a bridesmaid?"

"Now you sound like Mum and Sarah. Get out of bed. It's time to go to the hospital. You have work to do."

Daniel heard the grin in Lexi's voice. "Yes, I do. And for a change it has nothing to do with sick children."

He said goodbye with a smile and severed the connection. With the help of his sister, Daniel was about to change his own future and that of his best friend, the woman he loved, irrevocably.

"Hold on tight, Amy Morgan," he said out loud. "You're in for the ride of your life."

Chapter Two

Daniel sat at a café table on the Tamarama beachside promenade in Sydney. Ever aware of the possibility of a good photograph, he scanned his surroundings with a practiced eye. On the steep concrete driveway leading down from the road, he found what he was looking for. His heart beat a little faster and his body tightened in anticipation.

She was stunning. He caught a glimpse of a shapely leg between her skirt and the long black boots of her professionally matched outfit. But it was the high, round breasts and fuck-me curves that really grabbed his attention.

Her long, straight hair streamed behind her in the breeze, the glare from the winter sun tinting it a coppery brown. Sunglasses, perched on a small button nose, hid her eyes. Full lips moved seductively as she spoke into her cell phone.

His groin stirred.

He lifted his ever-present camera as his photographer's instincts took over and zoomed in, focusing on the flawless skin of her face. He waited until she faced him, stared at his lens before he took the photograph. Several more were taken in quick succession, capturing her startled look, then annoyance, then finally determination, highlighted by the purse of her lips and set of her jaw.

She was pissed off.

He watched through his Nikon lens as she clicked her phone shut and marched over to him. When she stood a few steps away, her proximity blurred the image, forcing him to lower the camera. She was close enough that the scent of vanilla, fresh and subtle, hit his nose.

"Did you just take a photo of me?" Her voice was soft and sexy and very irritated.

He smiled unabashedly in an attempt to disarm her. "I did." Her aroma continued to waft around him, through him, and he had to adjust his position as his jeans stretched taut around his growing erection.

She pulled a chair out from the table and sat down. Her eyes narrowed. "It didn't occur to you to ask my permission?"

"Nope." He leaned forward an inch, loath to lose her scent.

Resting her arms on the table, she said, "Do you think that's fair?"

"Yup. With those looks, you should be a model." She was any photographer's dream subject. He could think of a few choice poses he'd like to film her in. None of them included clothes.

She frowned. "I don't like having my picture taken. Please put the camera away."

"Sorry," he said in the nicest possible way. "Can't do that." All he had on film was her face. He wanted the body too. And the legs—the endlessly long legs in those foxy, high-heeled boots. Legs he'd like wrapped around his waist as they made love. She could leave the boots on—everything else would have to come off.

"C'mon Dan. You know how uncomfortable I get. Just put the camera down and let's have lunch."

"Morgan," he said, addressing her by her last name as he

always did. "I've been taking pictures of you for years. Your face was made for a camera. Don't you think it's time you accepted that I'm not going to stop?"

"I think you take advantage of the fact I'm your best friend and as such, won't scream at you." Amy pouted.

He laughed even as his lips itched to taste the full-mouthed pout. "Yeah, right. You never scream. Or lecture, or tell me when I'm doing something you don't like."

Her face relaxed into a smile. "Okay, so maybe I scream at you every now and again, but it's not as if you listen anyway."

A waitress delivered their food, interrupting their conversation. "Hope you don't mind," he told Amy, "but you said you were in a hurry, so I ordered for us."

The waitress leaned over, offering Daniel an impressive view of her cleavage, and cast him a suggestive glance. He merely smiled and directed his attention back to his friend. Once upon a time he would have accepted the invitation. Not now.

"Thanks," Amy answered as she watched the waitress strut off. She looked at him with a bemused smile. "I still get a kick out of watching women try to pick you up."

Daniel shrugged. "What can I say? I'm a good-looking guy. Everyone wants a piece of me." He chuckled out loud. *Everyone except you.*

She bit into her bruschetta and a look of ecstasy flitted across her face. "Mmm... You know this is my favorite."

For a full thirty seconds he was winded. She had that exact look on her face in his dream last night. Need rolled through him. He tucked into his own meal, hoping the bread and soup would satisfy the hunger gnawing away at him. It didn't. His cock was so hard it hurt.

He cleared his throat. "Do me a favor?"

"Name it."

He lifted his camera. "Go stand there against the railing and watch the surfers for a couple of minutes." He was taking a chance, but it was worth it if he could get a shot of her from behind. She had a great ass—round and tight.

"You're impossible!"

"I know. You'll do it anyway, won't you?" He flashed a smile, one he knew she couldn't say no to.

Instead of complying like he expected her to, she ignored him and leaned back, sipping her latte. "How was the last day of your shoot at the hospital?"

"You're changing the subject." He smiled again, a pleading smile this time.

"Your lunch is getting cold. And your dimples don't work on me, so lose the smile. Besides, I have to be back at the office in forty-five minutes so it doesn't give us much time."

Resigned to the unhappy fact that Amy wouldn't pose for him today, Daniel put his camera away, sighing.

"So how did your last day go?" The teasing note in her voice was now gone.

Daniel thought for a minute. "Bittersweet, I guess. I'm glad the shoot's over. I can focus on developing the prints. But, shit," he shook his head as emotion clawed at his gut, "it was hard to say goodbye to some of the kids."

"You'll go back and visit them, won't you?"

"Yeah, of course." His voice caught and he had to clear his throat. "I'm just not sure which of them will be there next time I go."

Amy nodded empathically. "This project's been hard on you."

"Very." He knew she understood why. After so many years of friendship, there were no secrets between them. Well, almost no secrets. Apart from the one tiny fact that he was wildly in love with her, Amy knew everything about him. But how could he confess the truth without her heading straight for the hills in abject terror?

"It's been rewarding too," he said. "I learned an amazing amount from the kids. Stuff that changed my way of thinking." *Understatement!* The last three months had brought back his past and in doing so, reshaped his future. He was a different person from the man he had been twelve weeks ago.

"Tell me about it."

Daniel hesitated a moment, thinking about the shoot, how much to tell her. He'd spent the last three months in the Pediatric Oncology and Hematology Ward at Sydney's Eastern Suburbs Hospital—POWS as the staff called it—capturing the children, their families and the staff members on film. His photos were being displayed in an exhibition that Lexi, a social worker on the ward, had organized. The funds raised from the exhibition would be used to upgrade and refurbish the ward.

It was no coincidence that Daniel and Lexi chose this particular project. The siblings had a special interest in children with cancer. When they were just kids themselves, their sister, Sarah, had been diagnosed with leukemia. It had been a year of pure hell but Sarah beat the odds and the cancer went into full remission.

It wasn't the assignment Daniel was reluctant to discuss with Amy—she knew all about it anyway. It was the consequences of the time he spent there. The lessons he learned that were so hard to share.

It was the terrifying moments of clarity that he couldn't voice just yet. How could he describe his emotion when watching a family spend their last precious hours with their son and brother? How could he share all he learned about himself while sitting beside the desperately ill young Vicky?

Vicky had gone home. The young boy hadn't. Their outcomes had been dramatically different. Twenty-odd years before, Daniel and his family had lived in fear that they were spending their last days with Sarah. They'd been fortunate. Unlike the boy, Sarah had survived.

Instead of answering Amy immediately, he reached for his bag and removed an envelope of photos he'd developed that morning. Flipping through them, he found one he was sought and handed it to his friend.

The black and white print was appropriate for the subject— a young, bald girl with dark eyes. The lack of color in the picture could not detract from the pasty shade of her skin.

"Her name's Vicky Campen. She's ten and has leukemia," he explained as Amy gazed at the picture. "She tried to smile for my camera, but a bout of nausea knocked her flat." He gnawed on his lip. His hand had been shaking when he took the shot.

He frowned, forming his sentences carefully. "She reminded me so much of Sarah." He tapped his fingers on the table. "I...we got pretty close while I was there. I spent a lot of time with her, just hanging out, talking, reading books. Then one day we had a chat about her illness." He tapped a little faster. "She spoke so candidly about the possibility she might die." He pictured Vicky's face at the time, recalled the adult eyes staring out from the child's face. "She just wanted a little more time to appreciate her family and the other people she loves. She's fighting her cancer so she can spend time with them. She learned she can't take anyone for granted." He stopped, stilled his fingers and took a deep breath. "Got me thinking...I do that a lot. Take my life and the people in it for granted."

Amy's expression was gentle as she looked at him. "I can't begin to imagine how difficult it must have been for you, spending all that time with Vicky. How many memories it must have brought back. But what you're saying is simply not true. I've never seen you take your friends or family for granted. And I think I can speak from experience."

"See, that's just the thing. I also never used to think that about myself. But Vicky forced me to look at my life and my behavior quite thoroughly. The truth is I'm not happy with where I am right now."

Her brow puckered as concern radiated from her. "Can you be more specific? What exactly aren't you happy with? Where would you rather be?"

He smiled. "Truthfully? I'm not ready to speak about it." The things he wanted to tell her would change the dynamics of their relationship and she wasn't ready to hear them. Not yet. Not until he'd put his plan into action.

Amy pushed her sunglasses up until they rested above her forehead. Brilliant green eyes appraised him and her face shone with curiosity. "I've been told I'm a good listener, you know."

He grinned at her, suddenly feeling horny as hell. Christ, he wanted to get her into bed, wanted to see those green eyes glazed with passion. "You'd be a pretty useless counselor if you weren't."

"Forget my job, we're talking about yours. Or about your life anyway. So come on. Where would you rather be?"

Oh God. She should only know where he wanted to be right now. Buried deep inside her slick, hot folds. Riding high on the wave of yet another orgasm. Locked away in a place where he could ravish her body at will...

"Daniel?" Amy's voice brought him back to the present. "You've got a funny look on your face. You okay?"

He looked at her. Oh, to just come right out and say it. To tell her how he felt. But he couldn't. She'd bolt if he did. Instead, he chose to appeal to her understanding, nurturing side. "I need a little time with this one, Morgan. I have to sort it out in my own mind first." He drummed his fingers on the table again. "I promise, when the time's right, we'll talk about it. Today though, I'd just like to sit here and enjoy my lunch with you."

Her face softened momentarily and she nodded. Then she shot him a suspicious look. "In other words, you want to see how much of my food I'll eat and if there'll be any left over for you."

"You don't think I'm here to enjoy your company?" He feigned hurt and injury.

"I think you enjoy the company of my bruschetta more. I don't understand why you don't just order two meals for yourself. You always end up eating half of mine anyway."

He smiled at her good-natured griping. "Ah, Morgan," he said. "It's nice to spend some quality time with you."

"It would be nicer if you told me your secrets," she replied before biting into her lunch.

He smiled again and a comfortable warmth settled over him. "I promise I'll tell you my secrets—" *When making love with me will be your first priority. When the only thing you can think about is me. When your sweet body is sated by my mouth and my hands and my cock. When resistance to me is a foreign concept.*

He looked her dead in the eye. "When the time's right."

Amy took another sip of her coffee and stared thoughtfully at her friend. Damn, he was hot. Handsome, charming and sexier than a pin-up model. She'd watched women drool over his honey-blond curls and sky-blue eyes. His devilish grin and impish dimples only added to his rakish appeal. Sometimes when she saw him, her breath would catch or her stomach would flip-flop for no reason.

It hadn't happened in a long time. Yet for a fleeting moment she had an unexpected urge to kick her chair aside, stride over to the other end of the table and perch her butt on his muscular lap. Press herself against him and feel his erection grow and lengthen with every sweep of her hips.

She was sure she could get him to reveal his secrets then. She felt a sweet pull between her legs and licked her suddenly dry lips as she contemplated the thought. Hmm...even if he didn't reveal his secrets she might just head on over to his lap anyway.

No.

Seducing one's friend was a very bad idea—there was no quicker way to destroy a friendship. All the dynamics of their relationship would change irrevocably if she slept with Daniel. Things would be awkward. There was no way they could go back to being just friends after that.

Instead she crossed her knees, rested her cheek on her hand and worked hard at suppressing the damn flush she felt staining her face.

Her philosophy was simple. It was one she learned the hard way. Friends were always around. Lovers left. Case in point number one: Simon left her. Case in point number two: her father left her mother. Daniel was a friend. He'd always be around. Unless he became her lover.

She'd known Daniel long enough to understand his pattern of behavior around women. He had an uncanny knack of leaving his lovers. Not cheating on them. Nope, unlike Simon and her father, the man did not have a malicious, unfaithful

27

bone in his body. He simply did not have the capacity to sustain a long-term relationship. In the entire time she'd known him, she'd witnessed him loving and leaving plenty of women. None of them had been around for longer than six months—at most.

She wanted Daniel to stay in her life forever. The only way to ensure he hung around was to keep him as a friend. Period.

A while back she made a decision never to sleep with him. If once or twice over the years she had erotic fantasies to the contrary, well that was too bad. It would never happen.

Apart from the fact that Daniel was her friend, he was also a man. Loving a man made you vulnerable. It opened you up to hurt and pain. She was through being hurt. She could survive very well without men in her life, thank you very much.

Well, except for Daniel of course.

Besides, now was not the time to be drooling over him. Daniel was under strain. His last assignment had dealt him a huge emotional blow. He was forced to face things he hadn't dealt with in a long time and he was hurting.

Whatever was worrying him would come out soon enough. When the time was right.

She relented. "Okay. I'll let it rest. You can tell me your secrets in your own good time." She smiled and tactfully changed the subject. "How's Laura?"

He rolled his eyes. "Her name's Lauren. I haven't seen Laura in months."

"Laura, Lauren. Same difference. In the last few years you've had so many girlfriends I can't keep up. I stopped trying ages ago." She knew she ragged him mercilessly about his sex life, but he *was* commitment phobic and made no pretense to be otherwise.

"It's over. I ended it a few nights ago."

Unsurprised by his revelation, Amy clucked in sympathy. Another broken heart. "How'd she take it?"

He grimaced. "I tried to be as gentle as possible, but there was a lot of crying involved."

"She never saw it coming, did she?"

"What can I say? She wasn't the right one for me. Besides, I did tell her from the start it wouldn't go anywhere."

"Ah, Danny, my friend…" She smiled at him. "Have you ever told a woman it would go anywhere?"

For the briefest second his eyes darkened, turning the shade of a stormy gray sky. But then they cleared again and he grinned. "Not yet."

"You really are a hopeless case, aren't you?" She breathed a sigh of relief as she checked her watch, took a last bite of her lunch and pushed the remaining half of her bruschetta over to Daniel. Lucky she hadn't made the enticing journey to his lap a few minutes ago. His attitude towards Laura or Lauren, or whatever her name was, just reinforced what she already knew. Daniel was a love-'em-and-leave-'em kind of a guy. If she ever slept with him, his behavior would be no different. They'd have sex and then he'd leave her…like he left all his girlfriends.

She watched him polish off her leftovers, and as he licked his fingers, she couldn't help but imagine what it would be like if those fingers were hers. How his warm, wet tongue would feel as it traced a path over her fingertips and down across her knuckles. Up her arm and over to her chest, stopping to tease her erect, tingling nipples. Pulling on them, sucking until she could bear the sweet torture no more and pushed his head down. What sensations his tongue would elicit as it licked her clit, dipped into her—

Holy crap!

There was no way she would sleep with him. If she did,

29

she'd be hit with a double whammy. First she'd lose her lover, and then she'd lose her friend.

The lover part she could deal with—maybe. Losing her best friend was unthinkable.

Chapter Three

It was late Friday afternoon and as had become routine over the last five years of working together, Amy and her friend and colleague, Maggie McGill, sat companionably on the couches in Amy's office. Amy was a counselor at The Sydney Fertility Clinic and Maggie one of the nursing co-coordinators.

"I saw an interesting case today," Maggie said. "A gay couple want to have a baby."

"Men or women?"

"Women. They just want the facts right now. They're not ready to make any decisions. One of them will contact us if they need our assistance."

"Sounds interesting. Count me in for counseling if they come back."

"I will." Maggie nodded and changed the subject. "Up to anything exciting tonight?"

"It's Daniel's sister's thirtieth. She's throwing a party at Bronte beach." Amy checked her watch. "Dan should be here any minute to collect me."

"Brilliant," Maggie beamed. "I can get a look at that incredible ass. You know..." She paused, looking thoughtful. "It still beats me why you haven't slept with him. If I had such a sexy friend, I'd just want to spend all day shagging him."

Jess Dee

Amy shrugged. "The opportunity hasn't arisen."

"It's not opportunity you want to arise. It's his—"

Amy cut her off with a laugh. "I tell you this all the time. We're just friends. Period. Sex would kill our friendship and I'm not willing to sacrifice Daniel for a night between the sheets."

"He must be a stallion between the sheets." Maggie's eyes turned dreamy. "C'mon, admit it, there've been times you've wondered what it would be like. Sex with Daniel."

Amy shrugged. She thought about it way more than she was willing to admit. "Sleeping with Daniel would screw up our friendship."

"How?"

"You know Daniel. He's commitment phobic. He'd make a lousy boyfriend. He's slept with more women in the last year than I've slept with men in my entire life." Daniel's affairs never lasted. He once explained that long-term relationships weren't his style. It was the thrill of the chase he liked, not the consistency of a relationship. "I've already lost one man I loved," she told Maggie. "I won't risk Daniel's friendship."

"Simon's an asshole," Maggie told her. "He wasn't worthy of your love."

Pain sliced through Amy as she remembered the agony of Simon's betrayal. She would never allow herself to be hurt like that again. *Never.*

"I agree. Simon is an asshole."

Amy didn't need to look up to know Daniel was in her office. Not only did she recognize his voice, she knew what he thought about Simon. Calling him an asshole was about the nicest thing he'd said about her ex in a long time.

She hoped Daniel hadn't heard any of the preceding conversation. That would just be embarrassing. When she

32

looked up to read his face, she gasped and forgot her concerns. "Your hair!"

He'd cut it off. All his glorious, golden curls...gone. Replaced by a short, dark-blond layer of hair.

His look was rueful as he ran a hand over his head. "It was time for a change. What do you think?"

Amy studied him. He looked so different, so unfamiliar. "I...it's...fashionable."

"That's the best you can do?" He laughed.

"I'm sorry, I don't mean to be rude. You look good." He did. Quite yummy in fact. The short length suited his face, accentuating his good looks. It highlighted his cheekbones and straight nose and turned his eyes a shade darker than a clear, blue pool. And his dimples seemed to have doubled in size. "You just don't look like you."

Maggie stood, grabbed her files and muttered under her breath so only Amy could hear, "Yeah, but I bet he's still a stallion in bed." Then a little louder she said, "Gotta go. Cool cut, Danno. Bye, Amy." She danced out of the office, turned around and ogled Daniel's butt. "Great ass," she mouthed before closing the door behind her.

Amy smiled at the nurse's antics and walked up to Daniel. She needed to get a feel for his new hairstyle. Stepping up close, she combed her fingers through his silky hair.

Her breast brushed against his muscular chest as she raised her arm and she was shocked to feel her nipple tighten in instant awareness. Daniel's sharp intake of breath also shocked her. She yanked her hand away, breaking contact, and then made the mistake of looking into his eyes. They were now a stormy gray and she was damned if she didn't see naked desire burning in his face.

Shit.

His nostrils flared and his eyes hooded. From the look on his face, she had no doubt he had one thing on his mind and one thing only. Where on earth was this coming from? Sex never figured in their friendship before. There was an unspoken understanding that they'd never sleep with each other. So why was he looking at her as if his cock might explode out of his pants if he didn't touch her?

More over, why was the thought of his cock exploding turning her on so much she could feel the demanding tug of arousal between her legs? She shifted restlessly. This was all too much for her.

"It takes some getting used to." His voice was an octave lower than usual.

"It sure does." She wasn't at all used to wanting to sleep with her friend so much she ached. How would he feel, hard and aroused and embedded deep inside her body?

"It's shorter than usual."

She doubted that. She'd seen Daniel in his boxers and size was definitely not his problem.

"But at least it doesn't get in my eyes."

What the...? Oh God. He was talking about his new haircut.

Had she misread his desire completely? Was it just her conversation with Maggie that had her all focused on the wrong part of his anatomy? Must be, because looking at his face now, there was no sign of passion at all. Just a devilish smile and a sexy dimple playing on his cheek.

Feeling slightly foolish and very breathless, she stepped away from Daniel and squeezed her thighs together. "It looks good." *Too good.* "You look all grown up." She hoped her voice didn't sound as raw as she thought it did. On the pretense of a cough she cleared her throat.

Her last statement brought a bit of reality screaming back. He was all grown up and still not interested in a serious relationship. Once again she reminded herself that sex with him would be a very bad idea.

Was it just her imagination or had she been reminding herself of that a lot lately?

He smiled at her. "I'll take that as a compliment. C'mon, Lex will be wondering where we are."

They climbed into Daniel's four-wheel drive and set off for the beach. Amy took a close look at her friend. His gorgeous profile was etched with stress lines. "How'd your day go? You look tired."

"I am. I've been trying to get all the prints developed. It's taking time, but I'll get there."

"I hate what this shoot's doing to you," she fussed. "I've never seen you like this."

"It hasn't been easy."

Amy knew why this shoot got to him. Knew all about his sister's illness. Daniel had come to terms with the cancer years ago, but being on the children's ward had dredged up awful memories for him, memories he hadn't visited in a long time. Perhaps now, as an adult, he was processing information he hadn't been able to comprehend as a child: his older sister had come precariously close to death.

It was unlike Daniel to get involved with his subjects. Objectivity was the key to good photography, he always said. Identify, empathize, sympathize but don't get involved. This time, due to Sarah, he'd lost his neutrality and he was hurting.

"Do you have a lot left to do?"

"There are a couple of rolls of film left to develop, but I've done most of them. I still have to choose the ones I'm going to show and enlarge them."

"It must be difficult, staring at sick children all day."

"It is. Especially when every kid I see reminds me of Sarah twenty years ago."

Amy watched as emotion danced across his face. His lips were pursed and his jaw locked in a tense grimace. She felt his pain as tangibly as if it were her own. He glanced at her and their eyes met and held. Before redirecting his attention to the road, he gave her a half smile. They'd always been able to read each other's expressions and unspoken thoughts. It came from years of shared experiences.

"Dan, will you be okay?"

His blue eyes turned dark. "I'll be fine. But yeah, it gets to me sometimes."

"You're allowed to be sad, you know."

He pinched the bridge of his nose. "Damn, Morgan, it's all so unjust. These children are young—babies. It's making me remember how useless I felt back then."

"There's a difference between now and then. This time you can help. This time you're making things better." She reached over and took his free hand, winding her fingers through his.

He caressed her palm with his thumb, which surprised her. It was a rather intimate gesture. She stared at him but he seemed to be unaware of his actions, so she didn't try to stop him...despite the unexpected shiver that ran up her spine and left her breasts tingling.

In fact, she enjoyed the subtle massage so much her eyes closed and her head dropped back against the seat. She would have moaned out loud if he hadn't chosen that minute to park the car.

It was just as well they stopped, because she was seriously

considering moving his hand from her palm to her breast. She scrambled out of the car and slammed the door shut. For the millionth time that day, she yelled to herself, *Seducing your friend is a very bad idea!*

They made their way across the grass to a group of about fifty or so people gathered together. Some stood chatting in small groups while others sat on blankets scattered around the lawn. A table laden with drinks and food had been set up for the guests. Several people danced near a portable CD player. Robbie Williams blared from the speakers and the ocean roared behind them. The party was in full swing.

They helped themselves to wine and Daniel scarfed down a chocolate as they searched for Lexi in the crowd. Amy watched as a female form disengaged itself from a group and headed over to them. "Daniel, Amy, hi."

She waited while Daniel hugged his sister happy birthday. She'd known Lexi as long as she'd known Daniel. She was two years younger than her brother and looked like a feminine version of him—tall and beautiful, with tumultuous blonde curls that fell past her shoulders. She was just as charismatic as Daniel but while he was laid back, Lexi was frenetic in her style. No wonder Daniel had succumbed so quickly to her request to do the exhibition. She was one hard lady to say no to.

Amy gave Lexi a kiss on her cheek and tipped her cup in her direction. "Happy birthday. I hope you have a really good year."

Lexi raised her own cup and smiled. "Thanks." She turned to Daniel and winked. "I hope we all have a really good year."

"I'll drink to that," Daniel answered and they all sipped.

"Danno, you remember Jack, don't you?" Lexi asked,

37

pulling them into her group of friends.

A few minutes later, Amy had been introduced to at least fifteen people and her head boggled at trying to remember their names. A chilly wind blew a strand of hair into her eyes. She pushed it away and nestled into her jacket.

"You cold?" Daniel slid his arm around her shoulder.

"A little." She resisted the impulse to burrow into his warmth.

Although she couldn't put her finger on it, something about him seemed different. Something was way more...*appealing* than usual. It wasn't just the hair, which the wind had now tousled, leaving it spiked at peculiar angles. Nor was it the unshaven look—dark-blond bristles shadowing his jaw line. It wasn't his clothes either, although no one could ever fill a pair of jeans like Danny did. They hugged his ass, reinforcing Maggie's assessment of how great it was. The navy jumper he wore set off the clear blue of his eyes to perfection.

Something about her friend was just...different.

"You know, I'm not used to your hair like that," she told him, "but I've got to say, you look pretty damn sexy."

"I do?" He looked at her with a surprised grin.

"Yeah, you've got that look about you, like you've just tumbled out of bed." A sudden thought occurred to her, one that would explain the unbridled sex appeal. "Oh! That's what you were doing before you came to fetch me. Who is she then? When do I get to meet your latest conquest?" Although she joked when she fired the questions at him, for no reason, she felt insanely jealous.

What the hell was going on? She'd never been jealous of Daniel's girlfriends before. Never. Maybe she felt a little off balance from her earlier attack of lust. Maybe that same desire was skewing her thought processes. She honestly didn't give a shit if Daniel was sleeping with a new woman. Did she?

"Morgan," he said with exaggerated patience, "I've been developing photos all day. I am allowed to look...unkempt. It doesn't mean I had a little rough and tumble before I collected you."

"Rough and tumble?" She laughed at his choice of words.

"Whatever. Let me assure you, there is no new woman in my life."

"My mistake then." Amy was unabashed by her incorrect assumption. Nine times out of ten she was right. She motioned with her eyes to someone behind him. "Lucky for that woman standing back there. She's been staring at you with definite interest." She watched as the stunning brunette eyed Daniel. The woman was tall with short hair, a voluptuous mouth and a killer body. Just Daniel's type.

He glanced around and cringed visibly. "Shit, that woman is stalking me." He edged Amy towards the CD player.

"Stalking you?" A woman who looked like that didn't need to stalk Daniel. All she had to do was send him a knowing glance across a room and her friend would happily respond.

"Okay, maybe that's a bad choice of words, but I can't get rid of her. Every time I turn around, she's there." He put his hands on her hips and swayed her in time to the music. "Dance with me. Maybe that'll put her off."

Amy let the music flow through her, trying to ignore the heat pulsating from Daniel's hands. "You're trying to avoid her?" She was incredulous. "That's so unlike you. She's gorgeous."

"Yeah, well that's not all she is." Daniel grimaced.

"What do you mean?"

"It's a long story.

"I've got time."

He shifted slightly. "This is awkward."

"Oh please," Amy scoffed. "You don't do awkward. Not when it comes to gorgeous women. Come on, 'fess up. Who is she?"

He danced a little closer and spoke a little softer. "Okay, but don't go making a big deal about it," he relented. "Her name's Leona Ramsey and she's one of the pediatricians at POWS. Ever since I walked into the ward she's been hitting on me. At first I was complimented by her behavior, but after a while it got to be a bit much. She started to become explicit in what she wanted." He shook his head. "It's bad, Morgan. She won't give up and I'm not interested."

"You're not?" She looked at him in disbelief. Beautiful women always interested Daniel. Why should this one be different?

"Because she's married," he explained when she asked.

"Oh..." Okay. Married women were an absolute no-no. "Well, why don't you just tell her you're not interested?" she asked reasonably.

He gave her a funny look. "Don't be daft. Of course I've told her. She won't listen."

"Was your message clear?"

"I told her I don't do married women and I wouldn't make an exception for her. How much clearer could I be?"

A grin tugged at the corners of her mouth. "What are you going to do?"

"I don't know. Any suggestions?"

"You're the king of dumping women. Surely you have a plan."

"Not a single one."

They danced in silence for a while. Amy tried to keep her

mind on Daniel's problem, but found herself distracted by the sexy way he moved to the music. Bryan Adams slowed the beat down and Daniel pulled her into a loose embrace. They swayed comfortably together, although she began to feel a little too snug in her friend's arms. His cock was just centimeters away and the image she'd had of it earlier, embedded deep within her body, was just too recent. Hot liquid seeped into her panties, kindling an awareness that should not have been there.

Christ, she hoped Daniel didn't know what she was thinking.

"Leona's still keeping a watchful eye on you." The woman stood a little way away—her gaze hadn't left Daniel the entire time they danced.

"Damn it, I can't get rid of her."

Movement caught her eye. "You better think of something. She's headed over here even as we speak."

"Shit."

"Think fast!"

He swore again and then laughed in surprise. "Hey. I have an idea." Without letting go of her, he nudged her backward until they stood slightly apart from the crowd. He touched her cheek gently and his eyes took on an odd glow. "But I'm going to need your help."

Oh no! She didn't like where this was heading. He was caressing her face and her heart hammered with uncertainty. "Danny—"

"Look, don't say anything. Just help me out. Please?" He stared at her mouth with obvious intent.

Amy's eyes widened as she realized what he was about to do. But she didn't have time to protest.

"Humor me." He tilted his head and kissed her.

Daniel's lips were warm, soft and exhilarating, and clung to hers with a promise of a thousand forbidden pleasures. They left her dazed. The man had done some crazy things in his time, but this was extreme. Friends didn't kiss each other. Not like this.

She pressed her hands against his chest, pushing him away. He didn't budge. Amy pushed harder. "Stop it." Her words were muffled against his lips.

He trailed a path of tiny kisses from her lips to her ear, leaving her cheek tingling.

"Quit fighting me," he whispered. "I'm desperate." His breath tickled her ear and the erotic sensation shot straight to her belly.

She stopped struggling and gave the situation brief consideration. She was acting like a teenager. Her friend needed help. How could she refuse him? It wasn't as if this was a real kiss—just one buddy helping out another. Right? It didn't matter if her breathing was suddenly erratic, she was just winded from surprise. Right?

He kissed her again, only this time it was more provocative. He coaxed her lips apart, teasing her mouth with his tongue. Heat seeped through his lips and left her craving more. His tongue begged for a response, and he was hard to resist. She stopped trying and relaxed into the moment, kissing him back. After all, it was for a good cause.

Right?

His mouth should have seemed familiar. Kissing him should have felt a bit like slipping on an old sweater on a chilly night, all snug and cozy.

It should have, but it didn't.

It felt so damn good she sizzled. Hypnotic warmth seeped through her limbs and into her breasts. Her nipples puckered and beaded and swelled against her bra.

Daniel whispered, "Thank you," and smiled against her mouth.

He wrapped his arms around her and pulled her close, intensifying their kiss.

She hadn't meant to enjoy it, but God help her, it was heaven. Her eyes lost their struggle to stay open and she lost herself to the sensations Daniel's mouth stirred in her. He tasted of rich chocolate and expensive wine. He tasted good. Too good considering the fact the unique and tempting flavor was that of her oldest friend.

She tingled all over.

He curved his body into hers, fitting them perfectly together. His muscled chest rubbed against her aching breasts, sending sparks racing through her stomach and lower. Her arms quivered when he ran his hands down her spine and her skin prickled with awareness as his breath fanned her face.

Every inch of her friend was hard and unmistakably male. He was aroused, his erection solid against her belly. It seemed to grow with every lick of his tongue.

She was on fire, alight with need. Liquid heat pooled between her legs and she burned inside. The hypnotic warmth vanished and fire replaced it. Flames flared with every touch of his hand, every stroke of his velvety tongue.

She lost herself in his kiss.

Her hands found their way behind his neck and nestled in his thick, short hair. He deepened the kiss and she drank him in. It had been a long time since she'd been held like this, kissed like this. Daniel's mouth brought something back to life, a part of her she'd buried a long time ago.

She'd forgotten how good it was to have a man run his

hands over her body, to feel hunger rage through her veins. To ache, to throb, to want. Burning heat suffused her and settled between her legs. A wave of desire washed over her and she arched against him, flattening her breasts against his rock-hard chest. Needing to get closer, to feel every inch of his body against hers.

She wanted more. Wanted his tongue running over her skin, electrifying her body like it electrified her mouth. She wanted him to taste her hidden juices Drink from her until he slaked his thirst and hers. And then she wanted him to bury himself inside her and ride her until she screamed his name in ecstasy. She wanted him to fuck her until their rapture was too much to bear and they came together—on a tide of infinite pleasure.

And she wanted to do it over and over and over again.

She moaned into his mouth and he responded with a soft growl and held her tighter. The rigid outline of his erection pushed against her stomach. Heat zinged through her as time stood still. The world around her ceased to exist. All she knew was this man, his invading mouth, his state of arousal, and her own.

But then he gave another low groan and pulled slowly away from her. The air between them felt chilled and she instantly missed the warmth of his mouth.

"Amy…" He took several deep breaths. "It worked." His voice was a husky growl in her ear. "Leona's gone. But we're not alone."

With that she came crashing down to earth.

She stepped back, breaking out of the circle of Daniel's arms. They certainly were not alone. There were people all around.

She stared at him in disbelief and shock. What had she

just done? What had *they* just done? She was so desperate to feel him pressing against her, she'd nearly done him right there on the grass. In front of all those people.

"I...uh, we...that is, I...! God, I need some space. Please excuse me." She turned around and strode off, appalled at her behavior.

She marched onto the beach, her feet sinking into the cold sand. Stopping a few meters short of the shoreline, she struggled to get her erratic heartbeat under control.

Oh Lord, how the fuck had one innocent kiss turned so hot so quickly?

"Morgan?" She flinched when Daniel touched her shoulder. "Why did you run off like that?"

"Why do you think?" She struggled to remain calm.

"You're upset."

"You could say that." *I'm also turned on and frustrated.*

"Don't be. It worked. When Leona saw what was going on, she walked away." He sounded unfazed by the incident.

Leona? Leona? She was ready to sleep with him and he was talking about Leona? "Uh, Dan? Pardon me for sounding stupid, but shouldn't we have walked away too? Did you notice what just happened between us?"

He gave her a crooked smile, his dimples creasing in his cheeks. "Yeah. Who would have thought we could burn up the beach like that?" He plunked himself down on the dry sand, with his legs bent and his arms resting behind him, supporting his weight.

Amy stared down at him, astounded by his casual, careless behavior. Had she been mistaken? Was he not as blown away by their encounter as she was? There was no mistaking the fact his groin had been interested. What about the rest of him?

"Don't you think it went a bit far?"

He shrugged. "You knew the deal, Morgan. If we had any hope of convincing Leona I wasn't interested in her, it had to go that far."

She did know. Heck, she'd even given him permission to kiss her. Still, things got way out of hand. "Well then, did you have to make it so...intense?"

He looked up at her and grinned. "I think you had a hand in that intensity."

Blood creep into her cheeks. She sat down next to him, shaking her head. "You're not in the least bit put out by any of this, are you?"

"Why should I be? I was in a predicament. You helped me out. It got a little hotter than it should have. That's all."

A little hotter? Hell, the grass where they stood still smoldered. "But don't you feel uncomfortable about it? I do. I'm worried what this could do to our friendship."

"Our friendship? You think this could affect our friendship?" Daniel laughed. "Morgan, it was a kiss, that's all. It shouldn't make you uncomfortable. If anything, you should feel proud that it worked."

She gaped at him. He'd turned the whole situation around, making a fiery, sexy kiss into a non-issue.

She closed her mouth and took a couple of moments to think about his words. Relief trickled through her. Hell, if he could deny the intensity of the moment, so could she. Happily. She didn't want to sleep with her friend. It was a bad idea.

A slow smile spread across her face. "It really worked?"

"Yep. Leona left about a minute into the kiss."

Time may have stood still while Daniel kissed her, but Amy was pretty sure it had lasted longer than a minute. "If she left so soon, why didn't you stop kissing me?"

He grinned and looked sheepish. "I didn't want to. I was enjoying myself."

"Daniel!" Amy couldn't say anything else. She'd enjoyed herself too.

"Besides, I had to make sure she got the message. If I stopped the moment I saw her walking away, Leona would have seen it for the scam it was."

She relaxed again. "Well then, I'm glad I could help."

"I'm glad too. Thanks. I couldn't have done it without you."

"No worries." She stood, pulling him up with her. "That's what friends are for."

Daniel kept a close eye on Amy as they walked back up the beach together. With every step tension seemed to ease out of her body. At least one of them was calm, because he certainly wasn't. Shit, his balls were so tight and his dick so hard that if she so much as smiled at him, he'd come right there on the sand.

His arms ached to hold her again. He could still taste her sweet mouth, still smell her subtle perfume—and the perfume wafting up from between her legs. She was so turned on he could smell it. It played havoc with his libido. He had no doubt he'd have a hard-on for the next several hours at least.

While she'd been shocked by their embrace, he'd been blown away. She'd responded to him, come alive in his arms and it hadn't been an act. Her touch, her kiss, her ardor had been very, very real.

He applauded his five-star performance afterward. He actually made her believe the kiss hadn't affected him. But his casual stance belied his aroused state. He was half mad with wanting her. What he wouldn't give to grab her again, kiss away her relief, hear her moan into his mouth, and crush her breasts against his chest. Grind his hips against hers.

What he wouldn't give to make love to her.

He understood she'd grasped his fake reaction to their kiss like a lifeline. Her relief was visible now in every feature of her beautiful face. Smiling to himself, he allowed her the temporary reprieve. It wouldn't last long.

As they neared the party, Daniel noted that Amy was wrapped up in her own thoughts, so she didn't notice him scan the crowds through the dim light. She didn't see him catch Lexi's eye and give her a subtle thumbs-up. She was unaware of his sister's exuberant grin, or the fact she nudged the woman standing next to her and whispered something in her ear. She did not see Leona Ramsey turn around and smile at Daniel. And she completely missed his answering wink.

Chapter Four

Daniel turned up the air conditioner in the car until the icy blast numbed the tip of his nose—not that it was hot outside. His sweltering state was solely related to the upcoming night: the opening of his exhibition and the turning point in his friendship with Amy.

After their kiss a few weeks ago, and in keeping with his original plan, Daniel had decided tonight would be the night. He was going to alter the bond between himself and Amy irrevocably. There would be no guise, no misconceptions and no trickery in place. Tonight their relationship would change. After the exhibition, things between them would never be the same.

There was a lot at stake. If the press and public hated his work, his professional reputation would be ruined. This in turn would impact his ability to raise the necessary funds required to refurbish the oncology ward.

And if Amy felt even the tiniest bit threatened by the next part of his plan, she'd bolt.

Anticipation shimmied through him as he pulled up outside her home. His breathing shallowed. The next few hours would be critical.

Amy greeted him at the front door in a dress that almost brought him to his knees. The hot black number hugged her curves and floated around her legs—and did dangerous things to her breasts. She looked incredible.

Did she have the vaguest idea of how damn sexy she was? Daniel clenched his fists by his sides and stifled his need to grab her. He took a deep, calming breath instead as he followed her inside. Bad move. Her trademark vanilla perfume assaulted his senses. God help him...he wanted her. Now. Wanted to finish what they started at Lexi's party. Wanted to push her against the wall, shove up her skirt and bury himself deep inside her. Spend the rest of the evening ravishing her, making love to her.

"So, tonight's the night."

Daniel whipped his head up. "What?" How did she know what he had planned?

"It's your big night. How are you feeling?"

Ah...she was referring to the exhibition. "A little nervous." The show was only partly responsible for the jittery sensation in the pit of his stomach.

"A little nervous? You're wound so tight you look ready to snap."

"I'll be fine."

"Would you like a drink, something to help you loosen up?"

He nodded. "Yeah, please. Scotch, straight up."

Amy poured them each a whiskey then clinked her glass against his. "To my best friend."

Four little words and they left him winded. Maybe because she knew how important tonight was to him. Maybe because they typified how much she cared. Whatever the case, she took his breath away.

He tried not to stare at her. Luminous green eyes watched him with concern. Full, moist lips covered in a sheer gloss curved into a troubled smile. How would she react if he leaned over and nibbled on the corner of her worried mouth?

Would her breath catch? Would she surrender her mouth to him? Would blood pulse through her veins and moisture pool between her legs? Would desire build and pound through her, like it did through him?

"I've never seen you like this, Dan. You seem...I don't know. Tense doesn't begin to describe it."

He held his shoulders stiff, determined not to kiss her. Not yet. "I'll be okay. You ready to go?"

"Just let me grab my wrap." Amy walked out of the room.

Daniel followed her with his gaze and a deep longing overpowered him. The gentle sway of her hips and the seductive slit in the side of her skirt, offering a delectable view of her thigh, were so inviting he had to fight down the urge to reach out and haul her back to him.

He downed his scotch in one mouthful and prayed the alcohol would burn away his feverish hunger for her. The drink didn't make a difference. His body was in overdrive. The only heat that could touch him now was that of Amy pressed up against him.

Tonight he would hold her in his arms again. And the heat of their desire would sear them both.

Ɛᴈ

Daniel held the gallery door open and Amy walked into the cavernous room, its walls lined with his beautifully framed photographs. A huge color picture of a group of doctors holding up champagne glasses hung on the wall opposite the door. The caption underneath it read *All in Good Health*. The blurb below welcomed guests to the exhibition.

51

"A posed picture," she noted. "Not your usual work."

"Yeah well, it was appropriate for the purpose of this exhibition. The rest of the pictures are more natural." Daniel paused then added, "If you can call photographs of sick kids natural."

Amy was worried. He'd been quieter than usual in the car. Distracted. Now his voice was strained. Nervous tension radiated out of every pore.

She touched his shoulder. "Would you like to take a few minutes before you have to face the crowds?"

He gave her a tight smile and shook his head. "Nah, I'll be fine."

"I know you will. More than that, the exhibition's going to be a huge success. Just wait and see."

He looked at her with a tenderness that softened the stress lines around his eyes. "How is it you always seem to know the right thing to say?"

She shrugged. "How is it you always seem to know the right picture to take?" She could have said something more, perhaps wished him luck, but there were times when words just weren't necessary between them. Instead, she stood on her tiptoes and kissed his cheek.

Since their encounter on the beach, she was careful to keep their interactions touch-free. But Daniel needed her and she could hardly refuse him a little physical support.

She reached up to wipe the lipstick off his face and he trapped her hand against his cheek, holding it there. His eyes filled with an intensity she couldn't read and her heart began an unsteady pounding in her chest.

Something was different between them. The air was charged in a way it had never been before and Daniel's touch, once casual and friendly, now seemed...heated.

Amy wanted to say something, but any further conversation was cut off as a woman swooped down on them. "Daniel! You're here," she boomed. "Come with me. There are so many people waiting to meet you. I've organized a mini press conference to start in ten minutes."

He gave Amy a helpless look as Valerie Carnell, the gallery owner, whisked him away into the crowd. Amy waved him off with an encouraging smile, hoping he'd relax as the evening wore on. She hoped she'd relax too. All this nervous energy between the two of them made her jumpy.

She accepted a glass of wine from a passing waiter, took a few large sips and when she felt a little more in control, turned to the photographs. It was time to see what had affected Daniel so much over the past few months.

The pictures were remarkable. Daniel had managed to capture the feel of the ward with uncanny accuracy. He'd brought the clinic to life. Amy was transported. The gallery dissolved away and she found herself standing in the middle of the hospital, watching the bustling activity taking place before her eyes.

She saw nurses tending to their sick patients. The care they lavished on the children was so powerful, Amy felt an inexplicable need to try and help. Couldn't she soothe away that small boy's pain, ease the teenage girl's hacking cough?

Her heart twisted as she watched a mother sitting by her son's side, holding his hand while he slept. A book lay forgotten in her lap as she stared down at him, her face haunted.

From the corner of her eye, she caught sight of a doctor on duty. His shoulders sagged and he looked downright exhausted. She could almost smell the coffee that steamed from his polystyrene cup, misting his glasses.

For the first time, Amy had a real idea of how Daniel must have felt when his sister was a patient on this very ward. She blinked rapidly, forcing her tears away. God, what the young Daniel must have gone through. The fear and the dread he must have lived with. No wonder he hated speaking about that year. No wonder the memories were hitting him so hard now.

She had a sudden compulsive need to find her friend, throw her arms around him and comfort him. To take away the pain. Make the hurt disappear. Though she searched the room, there was no sign of him. He was probably busy with the press interviews.

With no other choice, she finished looking at the photos and smiled at the last one. A picture of a little boy and his father leaving the hospital. A huge grin and a bunch of balloons spoke of happy outcomes.

"Aren't they incredible?" a voice from behind her asked.

"Unbelievable." She turned around to find Daniel's mother, Molly, and his sister, Sarah. "Hello there." She was genuinely happy to see them. "Lord, you must be proud," she enthused, excited to have someone to rave to about the exhibition.

"Oh believe me, I am," Molly said. "I've been telling everyone I pass that the photographer is my son." She didn't look the least bit embarrassed.

Sarah cringed. "Believe her. She's been telling *everyone!*"

Amy grinned. "I know what you mean. I've had this mad need to nudge people and tell them Daniel's *my* best friend. Isn't he the most brilliant photographer ever?"

"Undoubtedly." Molly smiled indulgently.

"And without bragging, this is his best work yet," Sarah added.

Amy realized that despite the laughter, being at the

exhibition couldn't have been easy for Daniel's family. "It must be tough on you both, seeing these pictures, reliving it all."

Sarah shrugged. "Not as tough as it's been on Daniel. He really struggled with this shoot. I dealt with my illness a long time ago. Daniel never did. He just accepted I was okay, and moved on. I think that now, for the first time, he's realizing how precarious the whole situation was, and it's taking its toll on him."

Amy nodded. Sarah hit the nail on the head. While the Tanner women always spoke openly about the leukemia, Daniel kept it firmly locked away. As a child, he'd simply accepted the return of her good health and left it at that. During the shoot, however, he'd had to come to terms with just how difficult Sarah's illness had been for the whole family.

Daniel and Lexi chose that moment to join them.

"Things look pretty serious here. You guys not having a good time?" Daniel had a broad grin on his face and Amy noticed he'd cheered up significantly. In fact, he looked downright exuberant.

"Not really," Sarah answered as she wrinkled her nose. "The entertainment's lousy and the décor stinks. The least they could have done was hang some decent art on the walls."

"Don't worry," Daniel said with a straight face. "I know the gallery owner. I'll have a word with her."

They all laughed.

Molly hugged her son. "You've made me very proud tonight."

"Thanks, Mum," Daniel answered and left his arm around his mother's shoulders.

"Dad would have been proud too," Sarah said and they all agreed.

Daniel's father had died a few years ago and Amy envied the family's ability to remember him with such love. Unfortunately, she couldn't think about her own father in the same light—hell, she didn't even know if he was dead or alive.

"So," Lexi asked her brother, "how does it feel being the center of attention?"

Daniel couldn't hide his smile. "Not bad. Although my eyes are still burning from all those flashes."

"About time you learned what it's like being on the other side of the lens," Amy pointed out.

"Flashes are good," Lexi said with authority. "They mean publicity. And the more publicity we have, the more money we can raise for the ward."

"I don't think raising money will be a problem," Molly said, her indulgent smile back in place. "Valerie told me she already sold fifteen photographs—and that was an hour ago, on opening night. You still have the rest of the week!"

Amy thought about the price tags attached to each photo, did a quick mental calculation and gave a silent whistle. If sales over the next seven days continued the same way, they'd be able to refurbish the entire hospital, never mind just the ward. Well, almost.

She looked at Daniel, ridiculously happy for him. He was staring straight at her and for a moment their eyes locked. The room around them fizzled away. All she could focus on was her friend, his hooded eyes and that intense, unreadable expression.

Her stomach did three quick cartwheels, a summersault and a backward flip in quick succession.

What the—?

And just like that, it was over. "Sarah, I think Steve is

looking for you." Daniel gestured across the room.

Sarah looked up and waved at her husband who was beckoning her. "I'm sorry to do this," she said, "but it's getting late. We have to get back home to the kids."

Amy looked at her watch. It was close to eleven.

"Are you ready to go, Mum?" Sarah asked.

"I am." Molly hugged Daniel again. "Tonight was just wonderful."

Sarah kissed everyone goodbye and Molly did the same, pausing to squeeze Amy's hand before she left. "Keep well, my dear. I hope to see you soon."

"You too," Amy said, still slightly breathless from Daniel's look.

"I'm going to see what the doctors on the ward thought about the show," Lexi said, then added with a wink, "Don't worry, Danno. I won't let Leona near you." Chuckling, she walked over to her friends.

A jolt went through Amy. Leona was here? She hadn't seen her. What would she have done if she had? What was the appropriate behavior when confronting a woman who was after your best friend? Should she tell her how incredibly sexy Daniel's kiss had been? How happy she was that Daniel had kissed her and not Leona?

Wait a minute.

She was *not* happy. Quite the contrary, she was doing her best to forget the damn kiss. Wasn't she?

She shook the thought away and focused on Daniel, casting him a wry grin. "Have you seen her tonight?"

"Are you kidding? I've had to duck into the men's room three times to avoid her."

Amy laughed and hoped the sound wasn't as tinny to

Daniel's ears as it was to hers. "Our, um...little façade didn't work, did it?"

He rolled his eyes. "Not really, but I don't want to talk about her now."

"Anything you say." Amy looked around and realized for the first time since they arrived she was alone with him. She took his hands in hers and pretended not to be scorched by the heat of his bare skin. "Your family is right, you know? You should be proud. Your work is unbelievable."

"I'm glad you like it." He held on to her hand.

"I love it."

He brushed her palm with the pad of his thumb and her arm tingled.

She ignored it. "I'm glad to see the pre-show jitters are gone. You were so nervous before." For some reason, it was her who was beginning to feel nervous.

Without saying a word he stared at her, his blue eyes turning a smoky gray.

"Daniel?" His gaze took on a predatory hue and she found her reaction to it most unsettling. "Are you okay?"

He blinked. "I need to get some fresh air. Come with me?" He didn't wait for her reply. With her hand still in his, he turned and walked towards the balcony.

Chapter Five

Amy stifled the flustered sensation in the pit of her belly, demanding the unwanted butterflies perform their nervous dance elsewhere. She waited as Daniel swept aside a curtain, revealing a door she never knew was there. Before shutting it behind them, he pulled the curtain back in place, concealing their exit from view. It was deserted on the balcony, too cold for anyone to be outside. She took a deep breath of wintry night air.

Daniel's behavior was...strange, and for the first time she found herself feeling awkward, alone with her friend. He led her over to a shadowed corner and leaned against the railing. It was dark there, the inky blackness obscuring her sight of him.

"You okay now?" She definitely wasn't. A peculiar sensation churned through her chest.

"Almost," he answered, his voice low.

She shivered, though whether it was from a blast of icy wind or his gravelly tone, she wasn't sure. Blinking a couple of times, she waited for her eyes to adapt to the lack of light.

"You're cold," he said. "Take my jacket." Slipping it off, he wrapped it around her shoulders and tucked it under her chin.

His warmth enveloped her and the intimacy of the gesture made her shiver again. Traces of his aftershave clung to the jacket and she inhaled, breathing in his spicy, familiar scent. It curled through her nose and coiled around her heart, making it flutter.

"Daniel?" She peered up at him. He hadn't moved. His hands still held the jacket together just above her breasts and he was close. Very close. Her nipples pebbled and she forgot what she wanted to say.

"Yes?" His mouth was mere inches away from hers. The cloak of darkness lent a clandestine aura to their conversation and tingles chased their way up her spine.

"Uh...nothing." How could she talk when he was this close?

"Amy?"

"Hmm?"

"I'm going to kiss you." His breath fanned her face and her stomach lurched.

Hadn't she already told him? It wasn't right for friends to kiss. "You probably shouldn't." Her tone lacked conviction and her eyelids were becoming too heavy to keep open.

"Why not?" His body hovered against hers.

"Honestly?" She quivered as sensation drowned out rational thought. "I can't remember."

The tip of his tongue touched her lips and she shuddered.

"Still think I shouldn't kiss you?" His voice was a smoky whisper.

She shook her head. "I can't think at all when you do that."

"Do what?" he breathed. "This?" He flicked his tongue over her lower lip and she whimpered. "Or this?" He ran his tongue under her upper lip.

"Mmm," was all she could manage.

"How about if I do this?" He pressed his lips against hers for the shortest time.

"Daniel." His name came out as a soft moan.

"Amy?" He stroked his cheek ever so lightly against hers.

"Shut up and kiss me."

Their kiss struck fever pitch the instant their lips met. Heat seared through her as she opened her mouth and he plunged his tongue inside. It tangled with hers, tasting, exploring, driving her half crazy with need.

If anticipation had drowned her logic, then his kiss immobilized her mind. Reality faded away. For the longest time she could only feel. Instinct and Daniel became her two guides and she blindly followed where they took her, heedless of the outcome.

His mouth was hot and wet and filled her with the most delicious sensations. The taste of scotch lingered on his tongue and she drank it in, unable to get enough.

He tightened his fingers at the back of her neck as his mouth ravaged hers. She wrapped her arms around his shoulders and was vaguely aware of the jacket draped over her shoulders dropping to the ground. Unable to resist, she stood on tiptoes and held her body flush with his.

As her pelvis made contact he gasped and backed her against the wall, pressing himself so close she felt in fine detail every miniscule move he made, every erratic breath he took.

And she felt his jutting erection just below her stomach.

"More..." She groaned and yanked his shirt out of his pants, the impulse to make contact with his bare flesh dictating her every move. He loosened his hold so her hands could creep under the soft cotton, up his sides and around to his chest. Her hands imbibed the warmth of his skin as she ran them over his muscular torso. The lean power contained there awed her, lending further credence to his undeniable masculinity. His heart pounded beneath his ribs, its staccato rhythm matching

61

her racing pulse.

Sweet Lord, he felt good. She grazed her fingers over his nipples and he jerked.

"Morgan..."

She answered by grinding her hips against him, whimpering as her clit grazed his erection. The clothing between them did little to dampen the erotic feel of his hard cock.

Moisture gathered between her legs and she groaned into his mouth. What little cognizance she had of the world around her narrowed until it vanished altogether. The only thing she was aware of was Daniel. Daniel and the way he touched her, the way he made her feel.

His hand found her swollen breast and closed over it, massaging until her breath came in short spurts. Her chest heaved as longing grew and blossomed, spreading its sensuous poison through her veins. When he took her aching nipple between his thumb and forefinger and squeezed gently, the sensation spiraled downwards, vibrating through her belly and lower. She stopped breathing altogether and was convinced she'd faint from sheer pleasure.

Daniel's mouth kept her firmly grounded. His kiss set her blood on fire. She moaned. She kissed. She ached.

With one arm wrapped around her shoulders—keeping her mouth fastened to his—he ran his hand down the length of her skirt. Then slipped it underneath.

Amy was sure her heart would stop. For an endless moment he rested his fingers on her knee. The anticipation of what would follow left her shaking helplessly. She was on fire, burning with expectation. Somewhere in the far recesses of her mind, a tiny voice cautioned her, warned her that whatever action she took now would have serious, long-term repercussions.

She paid the warning no heed, such was the power of her voracious need for him.

Touch me. Her yell was silent—she was powerless to find expression for her thoughts.

As if responding to her unspoken command, he dragged his fingertips up her inner leg, over her thigh-high stockings and onto bare flesh. Each inch of skin he brushed over was so sensitized his touch reverberated through her entire body. She turned to liquid in his arms.

"Danny." Her moan guttural, she shifted, inviting his hand to complete its journey.

An inch away from his target, he stilled and muttered a thick curse. A second later his finger traced her lacy g-string, his touch as light as a feather and as hot as burning coal.

She gasped at the contact and bit his neck. Tremors shook through her. She shifted again, needing to feel his touch on her naked flesh, the pleasure and relief his hand could bring.

He nudged the wisp of lace aside and ran his finger through her slick folds. Her head fell back, her eyes shut, and her mouth was incapable of speech. Even the tiny voice in the back of her mind was silenced by his strokes.

"God, you're so wet."

Wild with need, she pushed against his hand.

"So wet, I can feel your cream on my fingers."

She felt it too, felt the moisture coat his hand. His finger traveled upward, found her aroused bud and caressed.

Yes. Oh God, yes. She twisted in his arms.

He rewarded her by adding pressure to his touch. "So wet, I can smell your desire."

She wasn't going to faint, she was going to die from pleasure. Her fingers raked his back as she fought against losing control.

"You're making me so hot, babe. I'm so hard, it hurts." He thumbed her clit, massaging in small circular motions as his finger slid against her wet slit and delved inside.

Yes!

"Feel me. Feel what you do to me." Full of wonder, Amy moved one hand from his back and tentatively cupped the bulge in his pants.

He slipped his finger deep inside her and her muscles clamped down involuntarily as sensation shot through her.

"God, Daniel..." She couldn't complete her sentence. Her mind was overtaken by sensation. Instead, she closed her hand around his cock and began to massage it. He grew even longer beneath her touch.

"You know what I'd really like?" Daniel moved his finger out then slid it back in again.

The same thing she'd really like? For her to rip off his pants, duck her head down and take him in her mouth. To run her tongue up the length of him, kissing and licking and sucking until he lost all control and came in her mouth.

"A blow job?"

He growled in her ear. "Besides that."

She dipped her fingers below the waistband of his pants. His penis jumped and he pushed into her hand. It was a tight fit, but she palmed him, holding the satiny, steel-like shaft. "No." Her voice was huskier than usual. "Tell me."

"I'd like you to come." The low whisper in her ear nearly did her in. His thumb circled her clit and he slipped a second finger inside her. She let out a strangled gasp and he caught her tongue in his mouth, sucking gently. He pulled his fingers out then slipped them back in again. Then again and again and again.

She thought her legs might collapse beneath her.

Her thumb brushed against the tip of his penis and she felt the milky drop of his pre-come on the head. Without another thought, she brought her thumb to her lips and sucked, the taste of his salty essence filling her mouth.

His movements stilled as he watched her, a low growl erupting from his chest.

With slow, controlled actions she licked her lips, then his. His entire body shook in response.

"You taste good."

"Christ, Morgan." He clamped his lips over hers, his tongue searing her mouth as his fingers renewed their carnal seduction.

She grabbed fistfuls of his shirt as he increased the pace.

"Come for me, baby." Daniel's voice was strained now. "I want to feel your juices pour over my hand. Come on. Come for me."

Tension built inside her. Pleasure grew and grew. Sensations swirled as his touch weaved its magic. She was alight, on fire, about as hot as she'd ever been. He increased the pressure with his thumb and drove in even higher. She could bear it no more.

Her pleasure peaked and her body tightened, her inner walls clamped down in a mind-shattering orgasm. Still he toyed with her, kneading and caressing as wave after wave of ecstasy hit her.

Juices poured out of her and she heard Daniel's satisfied words. "That's right, baby. I can feel it. Come for me, come hard."

She did. So hard, her knees buckled. She had to grab his

waist for support, otherwise she'd slide to the floor in a boneless heap. For several minutes she leaned against him, breathless, as the spasms subsided. All the while Daniel whispered encouragement in her ear, holding her close with a steadying arm.

As the euphoria of the afterglow began to settle around her, she remembered there was a not-so-small matter still needing her attention. Dropping to her knees, she gave in to her previous desire.

She wanted a mouthful of Daniel.

Now.

In record time she unbuckled his belt and slid his zipper down. She eased his cock out of his boxers, felt it twitch. She licked her lips in anticipation and then licked the tip of his cock. Hunger overtook her and she indulged herself. Greedy for him, her tongue repeatedly laved his shaft and then twirled around its head, lapping away another bead of semen.

God, he tasted good. Salty and masculine.

Low moans filled her ears, urging her on, his fingers woven through her hair.

She wrapped her hand around the base of his cock and took a second to look at his face. His head was thrown back, his eyes narrowed slits. Even in the dark she could see the desire in his expression. She smiled, opened her mouth and closed it over him. A muffled groan sounded above her.

"Christ...Amy."

Forming a tight, wet cavern with her mouth, she sucked him, loving his taste and his feel. Loving the shudders that wracked his body every few seconds. Her head moved to a rhythmic beat, her hand trailing in its path. As his cock grew in her mouth, she moved faster, sucked a little harder.

Daniel's breath came in sharp bursts. "Amy…"

She cupped his balls with her free hand. His body tightened and froze. With a throaty groan, he came, shooting come into her mouth. She hungrily swallowed every last drop, lingering over her feast until his orgasm subsided.

"Amy." His voice was low and gruff, barely audible. He pulled her to her feet and held her close. "Babe…that was incredible." He took a deep, shuddering breath. For a long while that was all she was aware of. The sound of his breathing, uneven and ragged, and the feel of his arms wrapped around her.

A burst of laughter rang out from someplace miles away. It took a minute or so before the sound penetrated the fog surrounding her brain. When it finally did, reality hit her square between the eyes, the effect much like a glass of ice water. She yanked free from Daniel's arms and stared at him, shocked.

He grabbed her hand and tried to pull her back into his embrace. "Amy?"

They were standing outside the gallery, for fuck's sake. A few feet away from a room full of people and an army of reporters—all of whom had come to see Daniel and his pictures. What if somebody had walked outside?

"Morgan, what's the matter?" He still breathed hard.

"Oh my God!" She was aghast. "Oh God, Daniel." For endless seconds, she was incapable of saying anything else. Horrified, she whispered, "What did we just do?"

"We did good, Morgan," Daniel said, his voice husky. "Let's go do it again. Somewhere a bit more private."

"What? Are you kidding?" Amy struggled to still her pounding heart. "We can't do that again. Ever. Jesus, friends don't do those sorts of things. And they especially don't do it meters away from a very public function!" She had the most incredible orgasm at the hands of her best friend—at his exhibition. In return she'd given him a blowjob—right outside the gallery.

How the hell had she allowed herself to lose control? She was mortified.

"I'm not kidding." Desire burned in his voice. "We just did it and I want to do it again. Let's go." He grasped her hand again.

"Go where?"

"My place, your place, I don't care. Let's just get out of here."

"Are you crazy? We're not going anywhere." She jerked her hand away.

"Fine. Then I'm going to kiss you again, right here. We couldn't stop at a kiss before, so there's no reason this time should be any different." He grabbed her by the waist and hauled her against him.

She felt an answering jolt of heat. "Daniel, stop it," she bit out desperately. "We can't do this here."

"You're not giving me much choice." He rubbed against her, hard, and she nearly cried out at the sweet agony of it.

"No!" She struggled against him. "I meant we can't do this at all. This is wrong."

"There was nothing wrong a few minutes ago, when your body shook with pleasure. When you wrapped your lips around my cock and gave me the sweetest head imaginable." The raw sensuality in his voice slipped straight into her belly and bounced around, causing sharp stabs of longing. He was right. There *was* nothing wrong a few minutes ago. But now, in the stark reality of the moment, everything was wrong. For starters, their friendship was headed down the absolutely wrong path.

Panic set in as he dipped his head to kiss her again. She couldn't do this with Daniel. Wouldn't.

"No!" This time she was more forceful. "I don't want this."

His reaction was immediate. He dropped his arms and stepped away from her, his posture tense and face unreadable. Her body cried out in protest.

"Shit, Danny, please don't be angry." She had to salvage the situation, make everything okay between them. "We can't go there. Not you and me. We can't take our friendship to that place. We'd be walking through a minefield."

Run to him, her body yelled. Who cares about the consequences? But the responsible and cautious part of her mind was back, along with rational thought. Her logic was correct. Further physical intimacy with Daniel was out of the question. It would ruin their friendship. It might have done so already. "You have to understand what I'm saying. I'm terrified of losing you. Please," she begged him. "Please don't be angry."

"Anger would hardly describe how I'm feeling."

She breathed deeply, knowing exactly how he felt. Sated, sexy, stunned. Exactly how she felt. She reached out to touch him, to comfort him, but then thought better of it. Touching him would only ignite a fresh spark between them. Instead, she ran her hand through her hair.

"Look, let's just forget this happened. Let's go back inside and—"

"You want to forget this ever happened?" he interrupted her. "Forget that five minutes ago you were writhing in my arms, climaxing on my hand? Forget that you gave me a blowjob? That's laughable." There was no trace of humor in his voice, just barely controlled fury.

A fresh wave of horror washed over Amy. *They were right outside the gallery, and she'd given him a blowjob.*

69

Daniel did up his pants and tucked his shirt back in, shoving the top haphazardly into his pants. It lay disheveled and uneven against his waist. Even in this light, he looked untidy and out of sorts. She could only guess how she looked. Her hair must be a mess, her lips felt swollen. Her body still tingled in the aftermath of her pleasure. Heat burned in her cheeks and she knew they must be filled with color.

She reached over and straightened Daniel's shirt, tucking in a loose corner.

"Shit, woman," he rasped. "Do you have any idea what you're doing to me?"

Amy jumped back. "I...I'm sorry. I'm not thinking straight."

"Neither of us is." His tone was a little gentler now. "Come on. Let's go back inside. It's not doing either of us any good being out here alone. We can continue this...conversation another time."

He picked up his jacket and put it on. Touching her elbow, he led her slowly to the door. As he pulled the door open, warm air and soft music hit her square in the face, and the full force of her panic assailed her again. Her lungs flailed and the breath caught in her throat. A single wall was all that had separated them from dozens of people. She'd lost control, given herself completely to the moment and to the passion—and anybody could have seen.

Oh, dear God. What have I done?

How would she ever get past this indiscretion? Could she ever look Daniel in the eye again without thinking about tonight? Of the incredible, illicit passion they'd shared?

Even as the last tingles of fading bliss shivered through her abdomen, Amy seriously doubted it.

Chapter Six

Amy sat at her desk and stared blindly out the office window. Thank God the day was almost over and she'd seen all her patients. She was exhausted, and her mind was plagued with matters that had nothing to do with work—blond-haired, blue-eyed matters with skilled hands and intoxicating kisses.

A yawn escaped her as she rubbed her eyes. She hadn't slept a wink. All she did last night was toss and turn and relive her outrageous orgasm at the exhibition. And Daniel's.

She had a lot of time to think and rationalize what they did. There was only one conclusion that made sense. Sex. It was all just sex. She hadn't been with a man for such a long time and she was only human after all. She had needs. Daniel's touch simply reminded her of those needs. It was the touch of a man and not the man himself that had driven her wild.

But why'd he have to go and touch her in the first place? How had things managed to get so out of hand so fast? One minute she and Daniel were celebrating his success and then the next she was on her knees, going down on him. What the hell happened between them? How could she lose control like that? Damn it, why didn't she just say no? Or did she?

Distracted, she tapped her pen against her diary, alternately appalled by her wanton behavior and perplexed by her response to Daniel. To top it off, every time she thought about his hand touching her, making love to her—which was just about every other minute—her belly flopped over and moisture seeped between her legs.

God, she was a mess. Heat filled her cheeks as she relived, once again, the head-spinning intimacy of Daniel's mouth on hers, his fingers inside her. She dropped her face in her hands and let out a low moan.

"Sounds serious," a voice said.

Amy didn't bother looking up. "It's worse."

Maggie closed the door behind her and pulled up a chair. "You want to talk about it?"

Without lifting her head, Amy shook it. "Can't. I'm too mortified."

"Nothing could be that bad, could it?"

At those words, Amy lifted her head, knowing her eyes reflected her despair. "Oh Mags," she said after a moment of silent deliberation. "I did something so stupid."

Maggie's voice was soft as she asked, "What did you do?"

"I kissed Daniel and...well, let's just say things got a little carried away."

Maggie stared at her, perplexed. "And that's stupid because...?"

Amy sighed. "You know how he is with women. He goes through them the way you go through chocolate. Hunts them down, unwraps them, enjoys them and then discards the paper."

Maggie nodded. "You're afraid Daniel will do that to you. Enjoy your...um, sweet bits for a while, then toss you aside like an empty wrapper."

Amy nodded. "Exactly. He'd find someone else before he was even finished with me. Then there goes our friendship down the toilet."

"You're scared he'd cheat on you?" Maggie asked in surprise.

"Of course he would. He's a man, isn't he?"

Maggie narrowed her eyes in speculation. "What are you worried about? That your friendship with Daniel may be jeopardized? Or that he might be unfaithful to you?"

"Both," she answered without thinking. "First he'd cheat and then our friendship would be destroyed."

"Amy, are you sure we're talking about Daniel?" Maggie asked gently. "Or are you confusing him with Simon?"

Amy stared at her, dumbstruck. Simon hadn't entered her head. The only person she'd thought about for the last twenty-four hours solid was Daniel.

Maggie touched her hand. "Honey, that's not Daniel you've just described. Sure, he has trouble with commitment, but we both know he's never cheated on a woman in his life. Don't mistake him for Simon. He doesn't deserve that."

Amy sagged against the back of her chair. *Of course* that wasn't Daniel's style. Her friend would *never* cheat. "God, I'm pathetic. Nine months. You'd think I'd be over him by now." How could Simon still have such a strong hold on her almost a year later?

"I do think you're over him. I just don't think you're over the hurt. Yes, the bastard cheated on you, but don't let it destroy your future. Don't turn every man into Simon. That's not fair to you. And projecting your anger onto Daniel isn't fair to him."

It was easy for Maggie to say. She was married and in a healthy relationship. Her parents were still together. She never had to deal with infidelity and cheating bastards. Still, she was right. Daniel wasn't Simon. Daniel would never cheat on her. Nope, he would treat her like cherished gold—until he grew bored of their fun and games. Then he'd dump her and move on. Just like he always did with his lovers.

"Don't you see, Mags? Whatever the reason, I never want to risk my friendship with Daniel. I'm just not willing to give him up. Not for a temporary fling."

"Who's to say it would be temporary?"

She stared at her friend, not bothering to answer. They both knew Daniel only did temporary.

"Okay," Maggie conceded. "But don't you think last night the two of you crossed some line? It might be hard to go back to just being friends now."

"Hard, but not impossible," Amy said with vehemence. "Especially if it means I'm going to save a friendship in the process." A friendship that meant more to her than a fling ever could.

"And you think Daniel will accept that? He's no pushover. If he wants to make something of last night, he will."

"I'll make sure he doesn't." Amy reached for the phone. "It's time we spoke about it anyway. I'll be damned if I'm going to let one incident ruin a lifetime of friendship." She punched in Daniel's number.

Maggie stood up. "I'll give you some privacy."

"Thanks for listening."

"Anytime."

&

Amy waited on a bench on the promenade above Coogee

beach. The coldness of the winter evening seemed to have little effect on the activity around her. A group of noisy teenagers yelled and laughed as they ate fish and chips on the grass, while beside them a dad played soccer with his two sons. In front of her, the paved path was packed with joggers and walkers.

She checked her watch. It was still a little early. The sun hadn't quite set yet, the sky behind her was strewn with orange and pink clouds. She arranged to meet Daniel at five-thirty and it was only a quarter past now. It gave her a few minutes to think about what she had to tell him.

It was quite simple, really. Last night was a mistake. She wanted Daniel to be her friend, not her lover. Daniel left his lovers. He was faithful to his friends. She would lay her cards on the table. Tell him that nothing more would happen between them. Their relationship would proceed platonically. Period.

Maggie's astute insight about Simon had thrown her. She couldn't stop thinking about him. Was her friend right? Was she confusing him with Daniel? How could she? The two were so different.

Daniel was trustworthy. Simon was not.

There was never any love lost between the two men. They never saw eye to eye. But Daniel gave Simon a chance for her sake. Simon, on the other hand, made no effort to get along with Daniel. There were times when he even complained that Daniel was a threat to their relationship. He couldn't accept that she had a male friend.

That wasn't new to her. It was a recurring problem in all her relationships. Men were always uneasy about her friendship with Daniel. She'd thought Simon would get past his ridiculous misconception. Daniel was as much of a risk to their relationship as Maggie was.

It was ironic really that Simon was so threatened by another man. In the end, it was he who was the unfaithful one. After two years together, the lowlife shithead cheated on her. In their bed.

She shouldn't have been so surprised. Men cheated all the time. Her father cheated on her mother. Repeatedly. Until he finally just upped and left. Why should Simon be any different?

Because she desperately wanted him to be different. She so desperately wanted a healthy, long-term relationship—with a faithful man—but she learned the hard way there was no such thing.

When she discovered his perfidy, she kicked him out immediately. However, the pain and the humiliation lasted longer than the break up. A lot longer. Thank God for Daniel during that time. He was her rock. More than once he simply held her while she cried, her tears leaving great wet blobs on his shirts.

When the anger set in, she screamed and ranted and raved, hurling glasses and dishes at the wall, envisioning Simon's face everywhere they hit. Even that passed, thanks to Danny. He started serving her food and drinks with plastic plates and cups, complaining good-naturedly that he was sick of replacing his glasses every time she visited.

Slowly, the pain subsided and she started to get over the asshole. Now, nine months after she booted him out, she was upset all over again. Only now did she realize his infidelity had consequences other than the immediate hurt and loss. Because of Simon—and her father—she lost her ability to trust men. The fear of hurt and betrayal was just too strong.

Even worse than that, because of Simon and her father, Amy found herself questioning her trust in Daniel.

ℛ

For a few moments Daniel stood unnoticed, watching her. The breeze rustled her hair and once again he felt his groin stir and harden. Shit, all he had to do was look at her and he got an erection. A kid had more control than he did. This was becoming ridiculous.

He guessed Amy must have been home to change. She wore navy sweat pants and a matching zip-up sweater which hung open, revealing a tight white T-shirt underneath. The pants hugged her hips and showed off her endlessly long legs.

A somber expression haunted her face. Knowing Amy as well as he did, he figured she'd done some heavy introspection, gone over every detail of the previous night in minuscule detail and come to the conclusion that what they did was wrong. She'd have found a million reasons why they shouldn't have done it in the first place and a million more why they would never do it again.

That was okay with him. She needed time to accept their relationship was changing. Hell, it had taken him years to act on his own feelings. The fact that he existed in a state of permanent arousal was something he was learning to live with.

Besides, he'd only put the first half of his plan into action. The rest of it hadn't even begun.

Amy turned towards him as he took a step closer. Her eyes closed briefly and when they opened her face was a neutral mask, devoid of the pain he just saw. She stood up.

"You looked so serious, I didn't want to disturb you."

"Just enjoying the view." Her words were a little stilted, an obvious lie.

He said nothing and leaned over to kiss her cheek instead.

He found it difficult to pull away. "How are you?" His need to touch her was so great he tucked a strand of her long hair behind her ear.

Color tinged her cheeks and she stepped back. "Tired. It was a late night."

"Yeah, I'm pretty bombed myself." By unspoken mutual consent, they began to walk along the beachside path. "I didn't get much sleep. I was way too wired when I got home."

"Me too."

He frowned. She was so detached. Guarded and reserved in a way she'd never been with him before.

Then her voice warmed up and her smile broke through, bringing the sun with it. "I'm so proud of you. The exhibition was awesome."

Warmth curled through his stomach. Amy's praise meant the world to him. "Thanks. Valerie phoned earlier to say she was pretty sure all of the pictures would be sold by the end of the week."

"How does that make you feel?"

"Good. It gives me a real sense of achievement."

"The reports must have been brilliant." She gave a startled cry and stopped in her tracks. "The papers! I forgot to read the reviews."

Daniel smiled. "They weren't half bad." He handed her a copy of the *Sydney Morning Herald* he'd brought along and pointed to an article.

Amy read the headline out loud. "Award-winning photographer wins our hearts." She gave a low whistle. "Daniel Tanner's breathtaking photographs pulled on our heart strings and our purse strings last night at the opening of his exhibition, 'All in Good Health'. The talented photographer brought The

Pediatric Hematology and Oncology Ward of the Sydney Eastern Suburbs Hospital alive in torrents of color and in subdued black and white. There was not a dry eye in the house by the end of the evening."

She finished reading in silence then turned and threw herself at him, hugging him tight. "Oh, that's brilliant."

He enclosed her in his arms, returning the hug. Her breasts pressed into his chest and need cut through him, hard and fast.

"You're famous," she gushed. "You're a star. Now everyone will think you're amazing, not just me."

She had no idea what she did to him. Her guard was down, and she'd lost her reserve. She was his Amy again and she was wrapped around him, her body flush with his, burning him through his clothes.

"My biggest fan." His voice was hoarse and in the position he found himself, he couldn't hide his response to her.

Amy jerked her arms back and shifted on her heels. She held herself stiff and composed her face into a frigid mask.

He took her hand. "Babe, please don't pull away. Don't cut me out like that. Not after what happened between us last night."

She yanked her hand from his. "Last night was a mistake," she snapped, and then looked appalled. "Oh God, I'm sorry. I didn't mean it to come out like that."

The expectant uncertainty didn't stop her words from slicing through him. "How *did* you mean it to come out?"

"That's what I wanted to talk about, to clear up any misunderstandings." She turned around and stared out at the ocean. "I...that is, last night should never have happened. It was wrong."

Jess Dee

"It didn't seem wrong at the time." Nothing in his life had ever felt more right.

"Maybe so," she conceded. "But in the cold light of day things look a lot different."

"You don't. You look every bit as beautiful as you did last night." He needed to disarm her, charm her and combat any argument she might make, no matter how logical.

She swallowed. "I was talking about...us."

"You think if I kissed you now, it would be any different? Any less...explosive? You think nothing else would happen?"

"That's exactly what I think. We both have our senses about us now. Things are normal again."

He allowed himself the pleasure of openly ogling her breasts. Their *normal* had changed and he couldn't wait to prove it to her. "Come here." He kept his voice low. "Let's find out exactly how things are in the cold light of day."

She squirmed and folded her arms in front of her chest, but not before he noticed her breasts straining against the tight T-shirt. Her nipples jutted out, clearly outlined beneath the elastic fabric. "We don't need to find out anything," she said forcefully. "I'm telling you, things are different. Last night, I got caught up in the moment and I let it go too far, that's all. I'm sorry, it was my mistake."

He moved closer to her and asked in a whisper, "You think we won't get caught up in the moment right here?" He traced her lips with his finger. "You think if I kissed you now you won't feel that excitement again?" Her mouth opened at his touch. He ran his finger ever so lightly between her lips before slipping it into her warm, wet mouth, and then out again, mimicking his actions from the night before.

"I...uh, no." She stared at him with glazed eyes, the rise and fall of her chest uneven.

80

She was lying. He could see it in her liquid green gaze, and his body tightened. If she looked at him with those bedroom eyes for another second, so help him he would disprove her theory. Convincingly.

He ran his finger along her lips again. "Amy," he murmured. "Would you like me to kiss you?"

"Yes," she whispered.

"Would you like me to touch you like I did last night?"

"Yes." It was a soft moan. Her lips closed around his finger and she sucked.

He was so hard it hurt. His mouth close to her ear, he murmured, "If I touch you, stroke you, will you come for me?"

"God, yes."

Without warning, her head snapped up. He heard a crack as her skull hit his, felt her teeth clamp down around his finger at the impact. She spat his finger out of her mouth and swore as she massaged her forehead. His own head throbbed in pain—as did his finger.

She glared at him. "Damn it, Tanner, now look what you made me do. Ouch." She looked at her hand, as if checking for blood, then punched his arm. "Shit! This is exactly what I don't want to get into with you." Her voice gathered strength and she hit him again. "I don't want to get involved with you physically. Can you please—" *punch* "—just—" *punch* "—understand that?" *Double punch.*

Her blows didn't hurt him, and he didn't try to stop her. She was nervous and frustrated and needed to get rid of her pent-up energy. The next time she felt like this, he'd give her a very different way of venting her aggravation.

"Hitting me isn't going to change what happened," he said reasonably. "We're already involved. Didn't I just prove it?"

Jess Dee

Her hand clenched into a fist again, but after a moment's deliberation she let her arm drop to her side. "It didn't mean anything. It was just an outlet for our over-aroused emotional states."

"Bull," he challenged her. "Last night was a turning point in our relationship and you know it."

"No, it wasn't." She returned her focus to the sea and her voice lost its fervor. "We're still exactly the same as we were yesterday and the day before that. Just friends."

Fuck, she was stubborn. "If that's all it was, then why are you trying so hard to put our friendship back into perspective? Why do you feel so uncomfortable with me? You can't even look me in the eye." He gave her a minute to absorb his words. "You're scared because of your response to me. You didn't expect it and now it's got you all bent out of shape."

When she didn't answer he knew he had her. She was as wound up as he was and it pissed him off to think she was trying to minimize the effect their newfound intimacy had on both of them.

"Okay," she relented. "You're right. Last night wasn't a normal, everyday event." She studied her nails. "Let's just put it down to a new experience and leave it at that."

"Let's not." He put his finger under her chin and turned her head, forcing her to look at him. "Let's repeat it as often as we can and see what other new experiences we can have together."

Amy swatted his hand away. "We can't do that," she cried. "Don't you see? It would all just get out of hand and we wouldn't be able to control ourselves and we'd sleep together and the next thing we know, our friendship would be ruined."

"You'd lose control?" Images of Amy lying naked beneath him, thrashing violently in the throes of a wild orgasm, crowded his mind and he nearly groaned out loud.

82

"That's not the point." She grimaced. "The point is we'd have sex and as a result our friendship would be ruined."

Daniel grinned. At least they were on the same wavelength now. Hell, yes they'd have sex. Repeatedly. "How do you reckon it would ruin our friendship? If anything, it would make us a lot closer. Besides, it wouldn't be sex." His voice turned husky at the thought. "We'd be making love."

Amy looked flustered. "No, we would not. Because it would never happen."

"Why not?"

"Because you and I are just friends. Nothing more."

"We can make it into something more."

"I don't want to."

"Your words are telling me one thing, but your face is saying something different." It was. Her pupils were dilated, leaving only a thin emerald rim around huge black holes. Her mouth had softened into a full-lipped pout and her tongue darted out nervously.

Christ, he would give anything for her to wrap that mouth around his cock again. For her hot hands to caress his balls while she sucked greedily away, her tongue licking up and down his shaft. He wanted to come in her mouth once more and watch as she swallowed then wiped her lips in satisfaction.

She squeezed her eyes shut for a second and sighed. "Look, I need to explain something to you. Could you please just let me speak, without interrupting and without contradicting me? And for God's sake," she raised her voice slightly, "stop touching me."

Daniel smiled ruefully and pulled his hand back. He'd been about to wind it through her hair, pull her face close to his and kiss her. Ravish her mouth until she whimpered and moaned like she had last night. Until her body was on fire. Until she was wet and begging for his touch, and for release.

"Go ahead," he assured her. "I won't say a word until you're finished."

Amy bit her lip. "See, the thing is, you're my best friend. I can't remember a time in my life when you weren't. You're always around when I need you. I love you and I don't know what I'd ever do without you."

She loved him. That's what he wanted to hear. "I—"

She cut him off. "I'm talking!"

"Sorry," he mouthed silently.

"What I was saying is that I never want to imagine life without you. And if I...slept with you, that's exactly what would happen. You'd fuck me and then you'd dump me." She grimaced. "I know you too well. I know how you work with women. God, I've been through enough break-ups with you. You're just not capable of sustaining a long-term relationship."

She held up her hands as if to placate him. "I'm not criticizing you. That's just the way you are and if it works for you, fine. But that's not what I want from you. If we got involved, it would be for a few weeks or a few months and then you'd be off again, looking for another conquest."

His heart filled with hope and he smiled. "Are you saying you want a long-term commitment from me?"

"No." Her response was rather too emphatic for his liking. "I'm saying I want you to be my friend. Period. You're unable to commit. You would leave me and that would ruin our friendship. Because no matter how hard we tried, we could never go back to what we have now. A friendship unspoiled by sex."

Daniel felt like he'd been punched in the gut and swore out

loud. "First of all, I would never jeopardize our friendship. It's just as important to me as it is to you. And second of all, I would never leave you."

"I know our friendship is important to you, but I also know how bored you get with women. Trust me, Danny. You would leave."

"Trust." He rolled the word around in his mouth. "Funny word choice, since you seem to have very little trust in me."

"I trust you with my life."

"Just not with your heart."

"All I know is that you're my friend and that's the way I want it to stay. Call me selfish, but I'm not willing to let you go for the sake of a little recreational sex."

"You think that's all sex between the two of us would be? Recreational?" He gave a cynical laugh. "Trust me, sweetheart, it would be a whole lot more meaningful than that."

She eyed him warily. "It doesn't matter. I'm telling you this because I don't want last night to happen again. Sex would kill our friendship."

"It could also make it so much stronger." Hell, fucking her would be the best thing that could happen to them. It would be fun, it would be hot and it would leave them both so gratified, neither would be able to walk for a week.

"I've given this a lot of thought," Amy countered. "It's the right decision."

"For whom?"

"For both of us."

Daniel started to argue but she cut him off. "Look, let's just leave it at that. I've said what I need to." The look on her face told him she was not open to negotiation.

"That's it? What about what I have to say?" Even as he

asked the question he knew he had to stop arguing. Time, he reminded himself. She needs time. She was barely over Simon. Throwing himself at her feet now would scare the crap out of her.

"Can you please just not say it," she begged.

Daniel nodded slowly. "All right," he said. "We'll play it your way." Because he couldn't help it, he added, "For now."

The look she shot at him was deadly.

They were quiet for a few minutes, the air between them tense. Then she touched his arm. "Thank you. For not pushing the issue."

He shrugged and looked around. It was almost dark. "Come on," he said. "I'll walk you home."

Together they set off for her flat, which was a couple of blocks from the beach. They walked in silence, neither saying anything until they reached her unit.

"Danny—" she closed the front door behind them and looked into his eyes, "—I know I'm being unfair. But life without you would be too horrible to even consider and I don't ever want to have to."

"Believe it or not, I understand where you're coming from." One of the reasons he needed to move slowly was for fear of losing her. If she ran from him now he'd curse his hastiness until the day he died. He pursed his lips. "But you need to know what you're rejecting, what you won't have if you insist on keeping things platonic between us."

He watched her mind working, could almost see her brace herself for whatever he might say, determined to contradict his argument with a brilliant defense strategy of her own.

So he never said a word. Instead, in a whirl of motion, he wound his arm around her neck, pulled her close and kissed her.

He expected her to resist, to fight him off, but she didn't. Maybe she was too stunned. Maybe she didn't really want to. Whatever the case, her lips accepted his immediately and parted to give his tongue access to her mouth. Its velvety warmth seared him and played havoc with his libido. He'd been hard since he saw her at the beach. Now even her slightest movement played havoc with his self-restraint.

Her nipples beaded against his chest and he pressed against them. A moan escaped her and she deepened the kiss. Damn, the woman could kiss. His toes curled and his balls tightened.

Slowly but deliberately, he withdrew his tongue from the silky confines of her mouth and continued to hold her, to rub his chest against the soft breasts and tight buds. Looking into her glazed green eyes, he said, "Give me five minutes of your time. That's all I need. Five minutes and I promise I'll get out of your hair." He nibbled her chin and jaw line.

A soft sigh of indecision escaped. "This is a very, very bad idea."

He kissed her lips. "Five minutes, Morgan. That's all. What can happen in five minutes?"

Still she looked uncertain. He nipped at her earlobe and she shivered in response. He made a mental note to give her earlobe a lot more attention in the future. "Five minutes."

Again she hesitated so he nibbled her lobe again. As a result she nodded vaguely. "Okay, five minutes. But that's all."

He kissed her again. Only it wasn't her lips his mouth ravaged now. It was her breasts. Pausing only to push her shirt up, he dipped his head and covered her white, lace-clad nipple with his lips. Taking the bud in his mouth, he sucked.

The lace scraped her nipple under his assault, so he

soothed it with his wet tongue, hoping the combination of sensations would drive her as insane as they were driving him.

They did. Amy shuddered and moaned his name.

Before moving to her other breast, Daniel popped the front clasp of her bra. The fabric gave way and her breasts sprang free. He pushed the lace aside and stopped dead for a couple of seconds, merely staring at her exposed chest. A strangled sound escaped from his mouth.

Her tits were incredible.

He whispered his appreciation, and she broke out in gooseflesh. "Amy, your breasts...they're beautiful. Round and firm. And inviting. And your nipples. Christ, they're so hard. So aroused." He laved first one and then the other with his tongue. "Like me."

Her breathing became labored as she shook in his arms.

"I could spend hours kissing them, licking them. Like this." He sucked one breast. Kissed it, caressed it, nibbled the erect, pink bud while she shivered and groaned. His gaze flew to the clock. "But I only have four minutes left."

He got down on his knees and trailed kisses from her breasts to her bellybutton. The gentle curve of her stomach was soft and firm, the skin around it satin to the touch. Some other time he'd explore it more thoroughly. The clock was ticking.

Her pants sat low on her hips. He found the cord and untied them, pushing them down over her curves. Her arms fluttered at her side, a pitiful attempt to stop him. Ignoring them, he planted a kiss on each hip and rested his nose on her panties, just above her clit.

Her legs shook, a nonsensical word escaping from her throat.

Oh, man, she was so hot. He felt her heat pulsating

through her panties. Like her bra, they were white and lacy and barely covered the hair on her mound.

He had to taste her.

Now.

He stood and swept her up in his arms, marching to her dining table. As he kicked a chair out of the way, he settled her on the edge of the table and tugged off her shoes while pulling her pants off.

"Lie back, babe."

She stared at him, her eyes hooded. "We shouldn't be doing this. Friends don't—"

Three minutes and counting. He didn't have time for her objections. His finger traced a line over her panties from her clit to her slit, effectively rendering her speechless.

"Lie back," he whispered again.

With a soft groan, she complied.

Her panties off and legs spread wide, for a full twenty seconds he did nothing but stare.

She was a goddess. Her butt was perched on the edge of the table, her knees bent, her secrets exposed. A sex goddess. His balls tightened and he fought down the furious need to bury himself in her wet depths. God help him, he loved her, wanted to make love to her so bad. Her nipples were taut and erect and pointing skywards. Lord, how he ached to take them in his mouth again.

But first he had to taste her.

He buried his nose in her mound and licked her with the tip of his tongue.

Her reaction was so violent she nearly shot off the table, so he placed an arm under each knee and held her in place. He gently blew and watched her tremble as his air touched her lips.

"Daniel…"

He looked up and caught sight of her swollen breasts.

"I'd love to suck your nipples, babe, but I can't. I'm going to kiss you here instead." He blew again.

Her legs bucked under his arms. "Daniel," she breathed.

"Touch your tits, babe. Do it, for me."

He heard her breathing sharpen and watched as she whipped her head from side to side.

"Let me see you rub your nipples, pleasure yourself." He licked her, filling his mouth with her sweet nectar, and she groaned in response. "Massage your tits, babe. Feel how hot they are." He licked her again, catching the moisture as it oozed out of her. "Touch them," he coaxed.

When she did, he nearly came in his pants.

Delicate feminine hands cupped her breasts and massaged. Long fingernails, painted a sexy red, squeezed her nipples. She began to pant.

Blood emptied into his groin and he forced himself to take a steadying breath. He fastened his mouth to her and ran his tongue between her folds, dipping it in to taste. The tempo he set was at first slow and then fast, alternating between licking her clit and her lips.

Breathless moaning egged him on. Shit, she was so hot and aroused she could barely keep her ass on the table.

She tilted her hips, pushing herself up to meet his tongue and then relaxed back down.

Emotion boiled in his stomach, a mixture of love and need. Could his feelings for her be any more powerful? Could his need for her be any more urgent?

His speed increased as he heard her moans, watched her pinch her own nipples. She thrust up again and again, her silent incitement compelling him to add pressure to his kiss.

Damn, she tasted good. Like honey and cream and sex—just like in his dream. If his cock came anywhere near her now, he'd last all of about one second. But he had no intention of fucking her today. He was saving that for another time. A time when *she* asked for it. Right now he had maybe one minute left, one minute to remind her what she'd be missing out on.

He fastened his mouth on her clit and licked in slow, light motions, gaining speed and momentum with every gasp from her mouth.

"Yes," she panted above him. "Yes, yes, yes!"

He slid a finger inside her.

"Daniel. Oh God, Daniel."

Amy screamed as he slipped a second finger in and sucked a tiny bit harder. Her muscles tightened around his hand and she came, her juices flowing onto his tongue. Greedily he lapped them up as if it were manna from heaven, not stopping until the final spasm rocked her body. Until she lay motionless on the table, her legs hanging limply over the edge.

A quick check of the clock showed that four minutes and forty-eight seconds had lapsed. Before his time was completely over, he walked around the table, leaned over and kissed her soundly.

Five minutes.

For a heartbeat longer his lips lingered against hers. Then, reluctantly, he moved away. She lay there on the table panting and breathless.

"That, my love, is what you are rejecting." His voice was raw and uneven.

He straightened up, shrugged his shoulders and added, "But hey, if you just want to be friends, that's cool too."

Amy gawked at him.

"Gotta go," he said casually and turned to leave.

It took every ounce of willpower not to go back to her. Not to rip off his pants and sheath himself in her quivering, wet depths. Hell, it took every ounce of self-control just to walk to the door without limping.

"Maybe we can catch a movie sometime next week. I'll call you." He waved goodbye, opened the door and just before closing it behind him, whistled the first few notes of a tune from *The Lion King*. He almost laughed out loud when he caught a last glimpse of Amy's face, gaping at him in disbelief. For her benefit, he whistled the rest of the tune a little louder as he hobbled painfully down the corridor.

He knew without a doubt she wouldn't come after him. After that orgasm she would hardly have the energy to breathe. Calling him back would probably kill her.

Chapter Seven

Amy was happy. Nope, more than that, she was absolutely, positively, one hundred percent thrilled. It had been a month since Daniel had been to her flat, a month since he blew her away with his wicked, wicked mouth. In all that time he hadn't touched her. Hadn't hugged her, hadn't even tried to shake her hand. He hadn't kissed her. Not once in over four weeks. Not even a little kiss. Not even a peck on the cheek.

Daniel *always* kissed her on the cheek.

Not anymore. Now he was respecting her wishes. Keeping their friendship platonic. She was truly delighted. Except maybe for the kiss on the cheek thing.

Okay, so she wasn't crazy about the fact that when they walked together he no longer draped a casual arm around her shoulders. Truth be told, she felt a bit uncomfortable looping her arm through his, which over the years had kind of become habit for her.

Then there was the little incident last Saturday, when he was eating his lemon meringue pie. What was that about anyway? Their routine was standard. He would cut off a piece with his fork, eat half of it then feed her the rest and so on, until the plate was clean.

Only last week he ate the whole thing. The whole slice. He didn't even push the plate over so she could help herself. She loved lemon meringue pie.

Otherwise, she was over the moon about the way their friendship was getting back to normal. Really, just delighted.

True, it had been a little awkward at first. Okay, it had been downright excruciating. Initially she didn't know how to act around him. Couldn't even talk without stuttering. She just knew her cheeks had rivaled the color of the deep purple tulips that were starting to blossom outside. But things gradually started to settle. Now both of them were just fine. Happy as pie in their friendship. Everything was hunky dory. Except maybe for the kiss on the cheek thing.

Amy started as the phone rang, jarring through her thoughts.

"Hello?"

"Amy, is that you?" The voice was feminine and anxious.

"Yeah, it is."

"Oh, thank God. It's Lexi."

"Lex? Is everything okay?"

"Yes. Um...well no, not quite."

Amy went cold. "What's the matter? What's happened?"

"It's Daniel. He's had an accident."

The energy drained from her body. Spots dotted her vision and she struggled to breath. "Oh God. Please, no."

"No, no. Don't panic," Lexi assured her immediately. "It's not serious. At least I don't think it's serious. Daniel does, but then you know Daniel. He thinks stubbing his toe is serious. It wasn't really an accident. Well, I guess that would depend on how you define accident—"

"Lexi! What happened to Daniel? Is he okay?"

"Yes, he's fine. I think. He was kind of attacked."

The hairs on Amy's neck stood on end. "What do you mean, 'kind of attacked'?"

"Well, he was mistaken for an intruder and hit with a cricket bat."

Her jaw dropped. "What? Who attacked him?"

"See, here's the stupid part." Lexi's voice became sheepish. "I did. He was at my place and I hit him."

Amy's eyes widened in disbelief. "You mistook your brother for an intruder and smacked him with a cricket bat?"

"I know it's ridiculous. Daniel has a key to my flat, so if I'm not there, he lets himself in. He told me he was coming round, but things got crazy at work and I forgot. When I got home and heard someone in my kitchen, I didn't even think. I just picked up the bat and swung." Lexi sounded downright embarrassed.

"He must have been delighted," was the dry rejoinder.

"Well, let's put it this way...he wasn't very happy. He was fast though. Moved like lightning. Just as well, I suppose, otherwise I think I might have fractured his skull."

"So where did you hit him?"

"I just tapped him on the shoulder in the end. That's not how he got hurt."

"There's more?"

"Yeah. He was holding a glass of water. As he jumped out the way, he dropped the glass and the water spilled everywhere. When he swiveled around to see why I attacked him, he slipped in the water and twisted his knee."

The absurdity of the situation hit her and Amy began to snicker. "Lucky he didn't cut himself on the broken glass."

"Amy," Lexi chided. "It's not funny."

"Sorry. Where's Daniel now?"

"I took him home. He was feeling sorry for himself and didn't really want to spend time with me." She paused. "I guess I can understand that."

"Will he be okay?"

"Oh, he'll be fine. As soon as he realizes his injuries aren't critical. He needs some cheering up and I am not the one who can do that. He'd throttle me if he saw me now. That's why I phoned you. I feel so bad about what happened I hoped you could go over to his place. You know, see how he is?"

"I guess I could." She didn't have any plans for the evening and she had no doubt Daniel would be feeling thoroughly sorry for himself.

"Amy, you're a lifesaver. Thank you. I'd phone Mum and ask her to go, but then I'd have to explain what happened and I'll never hear the end of it."

"Don't worry about it. It'll be a pleasure. Besides, I'd like to get Daniel's take on the whole incident." She snickered again.

"Please don't tell him I phoned you," Lexi begged. "He'll just get madder at me for sending someone to look after him."

Amy shook her head in amusement. "Right, Lex. I won't say a word. I'll just pop in for a surprise visit. I'm sure Daniel won't suspect a thing."

"Thanks, I owe you one. Look, I'll call later to see how he's doing. Please, do me a favor? If he still seems upset with me, will you answer the phone when it rings?"

Amy smiled and gave her promise, then hung up. She was stunned to see her hands shaking.

Fucking hell.

Daniel had been in an accident.

Granted, it was a freak accident and he was fine. But still. *Fucking hell.*

She nearly fainted when she heard he was attacked. Visions of violent, masked men assaulting him, leaving him half-dead on the pavement, fighting for his life, floated before her eyes. It wasn't out of the realm of possibility. Daniel went wherever he thought he could find a good picture. He'd been in the middle of far worse situations before.

Lucky she was sitting down. The realization that Daniel might have been seriously hurt hit her. She put her head on her knees and waited for the rising nausea to pass.

She didn't know what she'd do if anything ever happened to him.

§

Amy pressed Daniel's doorbell and bit the inside of her cheek, her humor restored. She'd had time to recover from the shock and replay her conversation with Lexi over in her mind. It was a ridiculous situation—hilarious, really. Every time she pictured Daniel slipping in the water and going down, she started to laugh. It was important she kept a straight face or Daniel would know right away Lexi had phoned her.

It was a lost cause.

Coughing and clearing her throat at the same time in an attempt to regain her composure, she buzzed again. He was taking his sweet time to get to the door.

"All right already," a voice called from inside. "I'm coming. Be patient, why don't you!"

Slow, heavy footsteps sounded on the other side of the door and then it was jerked opened. "Yeah. What is it?"

Amy bit the inside of her cheek again. Daniel was not a happy camper.

"Amy? What are you doing here?" If he wasn't scowling so much, he might have looked surprised to see her.

"Good to see you too," she greeted him. "I thought I'd pop in and say hi. But since you look as though you don't want company, I'll come back another time." She turned to leave.

"No—wait, don't go. I'm sorry. I'm a little...peeved, that's all. Come in."

"You sure? You look like you'd prefer to be alone."

"I'm sure." The frown hadn't left his face.

Amy nodded and walked into his flat. She promised Lexi she'd see if Daniel was okay and she wasn't about to go back on her word. Besides, a small part of her needed to make sure he wasn't seriously injured.

She set her purse and a large plastic bag down on his dining room table, next to a packet of frozen veggies. She looked from the peas to Daniel and back again. Unable to help herself, she smiled. "Dinner?"

"Yeah. I was just about to pour myself a bowl of frozen peas," he said testily. "Would you like some?" He slammed the door shut and limped into the lounge.

"Have you had a bad day?" Amy asked innocently. "You're as touchy as a bear with a sore paw." *Great line, Morgan.*

"My paw is fine. Thank you for asking."

She eyed his leg. "Then why are you limping?"

"I twisted my knee."

"Ouch! How did that happen?"

"It's not important."

Amy raised an eyebrow. "Is it painful?"

"No."

"Then why are you limping?"

"Okay, it's painful," Daniel admitted reluctantly. "Happy?"

"It looks sore. How did you twist it?"

"Morgan, I don't want to discuss it right now. Suffice to say, I twisted my knee and it hurts like hell. Now, can we talk about something else? Please?" He grabbed the peas, hobbled to the couch and collapsed onto it. Stretching the long, injured leg out in front of him, he placed the vegetables on his knee and winced as the icy packet touched his skin.

Amy sat down on the opposite couch and scrunched her face up in concern. "That looks cold. It must feel like hell."

He eyed her with irritation. "It does. It's helping with the swelling though, so I can't complain."

"Have you taken something for the pain?"

"Yeah, a couple of painkillers. Now I just have to wait for them to work."

"So how did it happen?"

He glared at her. "Can you please just not ask?"

"Why not?"

"I don't want to talk about it. Now, did you come for a reason or are you just going to sit there and annoy me?"

"Well, I did come for a reason." Amy smiled. "But I think I'd rather sit here and annoy you."

"Well then, congratulations. You're doing a damn good job."

"Am I to assume you're not going to tell me what happened?"

"Assume whatever you want."

"Did you trip?"

"What?"

"Did you trip? Is that how you twisted your knee?"

"No," he bit out. "I did not trip."

"Oh. Were you tackled?"

"Tackled?" The look he gave her said more eloquently than words that he thought she'd lost her marbles.

"You know, like when you play rugby and your opponent tackles you. Did you go down and twist your knee at the same time?"

"You ask an awful lot of questions."

"I have to. You don't give me much to work with."

"For good reason."

"Yeah, I know. You don't want to talk about it."

"Why did you come here?"

"Good diversionary tactic. Change the subject."

"Amy..." Daniel fired a threatening look in her direction.

"Okay. I stopped off at *The Sushi Train*. I thought you might be in the mood for a little Japanese takeaway."

"You did?" That got his interest.

"Mm-hmm."

"You got me California rolls?" His tone was a lot less grumpy than before.

She pointed to the bag she'd set down earlier. "On the table."

"With extra wasabi?"

"Mm hmm."

"Oh..." A smile tugged the corners of his mouth. "Maybe you're not as annoying tonight as I thought."

"Is that a compliment?"

"It's a reprieve."

"So how did you hurt your leg?"

"Damn it, Morgan!" He lowered his foot gingerly to the floor and stood up. "If you don't mind, I'm going to get some water."

As he inched his way to the kitchen, she called after him, "Be careful you don't slip."

Daniel stopped dead in his tracks and turned around with painstaking precision.

Oops. Looked like she was the one who slipped.

"You took a chance coming here tonight." Suspicion laced his tone. "How did you know I'd be home?"

"Lucky guess?"

"I don't think so."

"You told me yesterday?"

"I didn't speak to you yesterday."

"Instinct?"

"Lexi phoned you, didn't she?"

Amy jumped up and hauled containers of food out of the bag. "I asked them to make you fresh rolls. I didn't take any of the ready-made ones."

He ignored her comment. "Your sole purpose in coming over here tonight was to make fun of me, wasn't it?"

"I came to comfort you. Lexi said you weren't feeling well."

"Aha! She *did* phone you. What else did she say?"

Oh shit. "Not much. Just that you'd had a, um...fall." Her lips started to twitch and a chuckle escaped from the back of her throat. She clamped a hand over her mouth.

"You know the whole story. You've known all along."

"Not everything. I think Lexi gave me a 'watered-down' version."

He rolled his eyes. "Funny."

"Okay, she may have 'slipped' in a few extra details."

"Yeah, yeah. Very cute"

"Aw, what's the matter? Is this conversation driving you 'batty'?"

"Lady, your sense of humor gets worse everyday."

A witty retort flew to her mouth just as the phone rang and she experienced a sudden stab of guilt. Lexi. "Oh, bugger, it's your sister. She said she'd phone to see how you were doing. Listen...don't tell her I told you she told me. She begged me not to. She'll kill me. In fact, don't answer that. I will. I'll tell her you told me. Yeah. That'll work. I'll just tell her you told me the whole story."

She grabbed the phone, keeping one eye on Daniel's now bemused face. "Hello?"

It wasn't Lexi. The voice on the other side of line was male and unfamiliar. She handed the phone over to Daniel. "It's for you," she said in a small voice, completely embarrassed. "Why don't I just get that water while you talk?"

She hightailed it to the kitchen and grabbed some glasses and plates. Okay, she admitted to herself, she was useless at keeping secrets. But at least Daniel seemed a little less tense. She took some water and a soft drink from the fridge and walked back to the lounge. By the time Daniel hung up the phone, she was eating her second piece of sushi.

"Nice of you to wait." Daniel hobbled to the couch.

"Yeah, it was also nice of me to get the food in the first place. And organize drinks and plates. And come and visit a sick friend."

He grinned. "You're right. It was nice of you. Thanks. Look, I'm sorry I was in such a bad mood. It's my sister I'm irritated with, not you. You were here and she wasn't, so I took it out on you. I apologize."

"That's okay." She smiled. "I quite enjoyed your misery. How are you feeling now?"

"Not bad, I guess. My shoulder's quite stiff though."

"Your shoulder? Lexi said she barely touched you when she took a swing at you."

"She was just relieved she didn't connect the bat with my head. D'ya want to see the bruise?"

Without waiting for an answer, he whipped off his shirt and dropped onto the couch next to her. He twisted around so she could inspect his shoulder. And what a shoulder it was. Broad and smooth and muscular.

Amy's mouth dried and the sushi she was chewing turned to sawdust. She swallowed the now-tasteless lump. Before she could help herself, her hand skimmed over his shoulder, relishing its warm texture and contained strength. Her eyes closed involuntarily. A month. She hadn't touched him in a month. An electric fence between them couldn't have stopped her from reaching out now.

"Can you see the bruise?"

Her eyes flew open. "Um...well, er..." She stared at his shoulder in surprise. "To be truthful, no. I can't see a thing." It wasn't a lie. Apart from the tempting flesh she had a hard time not nibbling, she could see neither mark nor blemish.

"What do you mean? Maybe you're looking in the wrong place. Here, let me show you." He reached his good arm round and grabbed her hand, pressing her palm down on the curve where his neck met his shoulder.

As her hand closed over his smooth skin again, she almost groaned in pleasure.

"Yeah. Just there," he directed. "Don't push too hard. It's a little tender." He pulled his arm away, leaving her hand to cradle his neck.

She ran her palm over his hot flesh, sliding it along with a feather-soft touch. Lord, he felt wonderful. How would he taste? She leaned her head in and opened her mouth.

An inch before her tongue made contact, he asked, "Can you see the bruise yet?"

She jerked her head away so fast she whacked it on the back of the sofa. God knows how she didn't get whiplash in the process.

He twisted around. "What's going on back there?"

"Uh...nothing?" Well, that was awkward. "Sorry, I still can't see anything." *Please, please, please, don't ask anything else.*

He didn't. "That's odd. It's so sore it's throbbing."

That was something she could identify with. She throbbed too. With awareness. So aware of him it hurt. She ached to touch him again, to run her hands over his body, face, lips. Kiss him. Dear Lord, she wanted to kiss him. So bad.

Crap.

All her well-laid plans to just be friends and here she sat, quietly simmering with desire. "Tell you what." She squirmed. Was that really her voice? That breathless whisper? "Why don't you pass over those peas and let me put them on the tender area. The ice should help with the bruising." If she could just get her hands on the packet, she could rub it over her neck and get her body temperature down below boiling point.

He just had to foil her brilliant plan. "Actually, Lexi stopped by a pharmacy to get some anti-inflammatory cream for my knee. Perhaps you could rub some into my neck?"

"Sure. Where is it?"

"In the packet next to the TV." He pointed to a white paper bag.

She retrieved the bag and pulled out a small tube, squeezing a blob of cold gel onto her fingers. Quietly reluctant, she sat down behind him again and pondered the wisdom of what she was about to do. Could she work her hands over the muscles in his shoulders and stop there? She seriously doubted it. There were other muscles she wanted to get her hands on but knew she shouldn't. Couldn't.

Bugger. How could she back out now without him seeing straight through her? Knowing the exact reason for her cowardice? The best way to keep their friendship on track was to just be friends. Friends helped each other out. It didn't go beyond the call of duty to massage gel into a friend's injured shoulder, did it? Even if it was the most unbelievably sexy shoulder ever created.

She rubbed the gel between her hands to warm it up before turning her attention to his invisible bruise. "Here?" She touched his neck lightly.

Oh boy. This is a bad idea. A very bad idea. Couldn't he just rub it in himself?

At least the medicinal smell reduced the temptation to take a bite of him.

"A little lower...just there."

She gently massaged his neck and shoulder, trying her damnedest not to relish the feel of his skin as she moved. Velvet-covered steel. She kneaded the gel into his knotted muscles, resisting the urge to follow the sinewy line down his back and onto his buttocks. The hard curve of his ass was just visible beneath his low-slung shorts. Visions raced through her mind of her massaging him there, rubbing and caressing before moving her hand around his hips until she found his cock.

She squeezed her hands into fists as she felt a tug of desire deep within. Shit, she shouldn't feel this way. Not now, not when they'd come so far. They were really, truly and honestly just friends again.

So why had her nipples tightened into little buds? Why was she so aroused—?

"Ouch!" Daniel's wince of pain brought her crashing back to reality. Her fist was clenched around his shoulder.

"Oh...sorry!" She stared at her hand, willing it to relax. "I was, um...distracted. Forgive me?"

"That's okay." His voice sounded strained.

Christ, he felt it too.

This massage was so over.

She gave a last gentle squeeze then stood up and raced to the bathroom. To wash her hands and throw some cold water over her face.

"Would you like some dinner now?" she asked when she returned. "You must be starving." She needed to keep busy or she'd just head straight back to the couch and resume the massage. If she did that, there was no way she'd just stick to his neck and shoulder.

"In a minute." Daniel turned on the couch until he faced her. He rolled his shoulders, testing for stiffness. Amy's eyes glued to the shift of muscles as they rippled beneath his skin. When he stretched, the sinuous movement pushed her restraint to the limit.

As he watched her the blue of his eyes turned a dark gray. "You have very effective hands, Morgan. I don't know what you did, but I'm not so..." He gave a wry smile. "My shoulder's not so stiff anymore."

How was she supposed to respond to that? Offer to take care of other stiff parts of his anatomy?

No!

She used her effective hands to pile some sushi on a plate and passed it to him, hoping he didn't notice the tremor in her grip. "Eat."

He watched her with a knowing smile but wordlessly accepted the dish, setting it down on the arm of the couch. Before she could pull her hand away, he caught it and turned it around, studying it, stroking it.

"Magic hands." His soft voice reverberated through her jittery belly. He held her hand, palm up, in his and ran his thumb seductively over it, using just the right amount of pressure to send tingles racing up her spine. The subtle gesture both relaxed and aroused her. Her arm went limp.

The air between them was supercharged.

He looked at her with dark, hooded eyes and Amy had to remind herself to breathe.

Friends. Friends, friends, friends, friends, friends.

With all the force she could muster, which was almost none, she pulled her hand away.

"Eat," she commanded in a whisper.

Daniel did as he was told. He lifted a piece of sushi to his open mouth and closed his lips around the rice. She'd eaten sushi with Daniel a hundred times before. Why was the very action of his chewing and swallowing now the most erotic thing she'd ever seen? Why the sudden urge to lie down, remove her shirt, put the remaining sushi on her stomach and let him eat it directly off her? Then encourage him to lick off the soy sauce?

She was staring. Gaping more like it.

Talk. Say something—anything. "You forgot the wasabi." Her voice trembled.

He eyed her lazily. "Sweetheart, I am so hot right now, a little wasabi would not make one jot of difference."

She swallowed convulsively. "Don't, Danny. You promised," she whispered. "We can't go there. We can't do this."

"We're adults. We can go wherever we want."

"Not together. Not us."

Silence filled the room. She stared at him, willing him not to take it any further and at the same time, wishing he would.

After an eternity, Daniel seemed to relax a little and a glint entered his eyes. "All right, Amy." Her name rolled off his lips, like a kiss. "We won't go there."

She breathed a sigh of relief. Or was it regret? "Thank you."

He winked at her and ate another piece of sushi.

Sizzle.

"Can I just ask one more favor?" He flashed his devilish grin.

Amy felt her guard go up again. "What is it?"

"It's my knee." His dimple played mischievously on his cheek. "It's starting to burn. I think it's beginning to swell. The pressure's radiating up my thigh."

She glanced at his leg. He was so not talking about his knee. It looked about as bruised and swollen as his unblemished shoulder.

"Morgan..." Daniel smiled impishly. "You did such a great job with my shoulder. Would it be too much to ask you to massage my leg as well?"

Chapter Eight

She would have given just about anything to massage his leg and Amy knew how she would've massaged it too. First, she'd push him back on the couch and bend his leg. Second, she'd climb on and straddle his knee between her thighs. Third, she'd settle back down and apply a tiny amount of pressure so that every time she moved, she would connect ever so erotically with his knee. Then finally, she'd gyrate, rubbing the muscles around his knee. Hell, she'd throw her life and soul into working that knee. She'd massage it so damn well he'd forget it was even injured in the first place.

Oh, for God's sake. She was fantasizing about humping his knee. Things had degraded beyond the point of decency. There was no way she was going to massage him again. Not his shoulder, not his knee nor any other part of his anatomy.

There was a better way. It involved Daniel taking off all his clothes.

"Tell you what," she said. "I've come up with another plan. Give me a few minutes to prepare." With that, she headed to the bathroom.

There was something incredibly intimate about drawing a bath for him. As she ran her hands through the heated water, she couldn't help but imagine Daniel lying here, his head resting against one edge of the bath, his feet stretched out against the other end. Visions of steam as it swirled around his chest and face raised her body temperature. It spiked even higher when she saw his cock float just above his balls. A moan escaped her throat and echoed throughout the bathroom at the vivid vision.

It was a good thing she closed the door. The last thing she needed was for him to hear her fantasize about him. She turned off the taps, walked to the sink and threw a little more cold water over her face and chest. *Better. Much better.*

Composed and body temperature lowered, she went back to Daniel.

"My mother always claimed a bath's the perfect place to soak away your aches and pains." She offered him a hand to help him up. "I want you to go and climb in. The water's hot and I've turned down the lights. I guarantee by the time you get out of that bathroom, you'll feel like a new man."

The question was, how would she feel, knowing he lay meters away from her, submerged in steamy water, naked as the day he was born?

Just fine. Just bloody fine, thank you.

"Thanks, Morgan, that's pretty decent of you." Daniel limped towards the bathroom but stopped before he went in. "Just one question."

"What?"

His smile revealed an evil flash of dimple. "If I have trouble washing all those difficult-to-reach places, will you come and help me?"

Choosing to ignore him, she switched on the TV, sat down and spent the next twenty minutes obsessing about which places would be difficult for him to reach, and how she would use the soap to make sure she got them *really* clean.

Fortunately the phone rang, interfering with her increasing obsession. This time it was Lexi and Amy assured her Daniel was just fine—his ego more bruised than his body.

When she hung up, she heard Daniel ask, "Who was that?"

"Your sister." She turned around. "She wanted—" Her tongue hit the floor, making intelligible speech pretty much impossible.

He stood before her wearing nothing but a white towel. It was wrapped low around his hips, the color accentuating his tanned skin. Below it, beads of water clung to the golden hairs curling on his long, muscular legs.

Water ran in tiny rivulets from his shoulders down his chest. Mesmerized, she watched a drop trickle over his nipple and slide down his hard, flat stomach only to disappear into the towel. Warm heat hummed in her belly and she repressed the urge to quench her sudden thirst by catching one of those droplets with her tongue.

God. He looked good enough to eat.

Desire shot through her. She wanted him. Wanted to run her hands over his wet torso, rip the towel from around his waist and devour him in all his naked, very male glory.

"Like what you see?"

"Huh?" She jerked her gaze up to meet Daniel's and saw amusement dancing in his eyes.

"Just asking if you like what you see."

Shit! She was ogling him and he had busted her.

What was she supposed to say? She *loved* what she saw? So much so she was almost as wet as he was? Not likely.

"I was looking to see if your, um…bruises were more visible than earlier." To reinforce her point, she lowered her gaze to his knees. The only problem was that her downward gaze snagged on the towel. Was it just her imagination or was there a bulge there? Did he have an erection, or was it just the way his towel hung against his hips?

"Are they?"

It certainly looked like an erection to her. "Are they what?"

"More visible now?"

"Huh?" It was most definitely an erection. A substantial one at that, given the way the towel just moved.

"The bruises, Morgan, can you see them now?"

"What bruises?" He was hard. That meant he was aroused. And if she was aroused and he was aroused, then—

She heard him chuckle. "A little distracted, are we?"

Bruises. Damn, they were talking about his bruises. *Focus.* She looked him dead in the eye and lied. "Not distracted, no. Just trying to make a point. I can't see any bruising." Well, at least that part was true. "Not on your shoulder or your knee. I'm sorry." She shrugged. "They're just not there."

He said nothing, raising his eyebrow instead. Her gaze hadn't taken in either knee or shoulder. The lift of his brow told her he knew exactly what she was thinking. But how could he not? Her tongue was still plastered to the floor. "You gonna stand there dripping all over the carpet? Or are you going to get dressed?"

"That depends." He didn't seem to be in a hurry to get his clothes on.

"On what?"

"On you."

"On me?"

"Yes. On you. Do you want me to get dressed?"

Hell, no! "What kind of a question is that?"

"A logical one. I saw you watching me. You just don't seem particularly eager for me to put my clothes on. In fact—" again with the infuriating dimple, "—you seem to have developed a certain affinity for my towel."

It wasn't the damn towel she had an affinity for. If he could just *lose* the towel, she'd be happy.

No. She wouldn't.

"Yeah, Dan. What can I say? I've fallen for the towel. I've always been a sucker for a good towel."

Daniel looked surprised. "You have? Well, I tell you what. I'm a nice guy and I'd hate to get in the way of you getting what you want. So here's what I'm going to do. I'm gonna go get dressed and I'm gonna leave you with my towel so the two of you can have a few minutes alone to get acquainted."

Ever so casually, he pulled the terry cloth from around his waist and handed it to a dumbfounded Amy.

"It's a little wet," he said apologetically and shrugged. "Sorry."

Amy was sure she'd have responded appropriately if she hadn't been so busy confirming her erection suspicions. The man had the granddaddy of all hard-ons.

"Wet?" she muttered. Forget the towel. The wettest thing in the room right now was her. She wished she had a pair of super-industrial-strength panties, because the longer she stared at Daniel's cock, the wetter she got.

Well, don't stare, then.

Easy for you to say.

Lift your eyes upwards, to his face.

I swear, I'm trying. It's just not working.

Daniel saved her from further self-debate. "I'll be back in five, Morgan. Enjoy getting to know the towel."

He turned around and sauntered off to his room, leaving the towel dangling uselessly in her hand.

It took longer than five minutes to get dressed. Daniel feared zipping up a pair of jeans in his state would maim him for life. He pulled on his clothes slowly, his lips twitching every time he pictured Amy's stunned face. Yep. There was no doubt about it. His good pal was hot and horny and ready to jump him.

And he just walked away.

Had he completely lost his mind? No reasonable man could walk away from a woman who looked at him like that.

But then Daniel wasn't exactly of sound mind. He hadn't been since he went down on her. Got a taste of her sweet sex. One lick and his sanity was history. Fucking her was the only thing that would help him regain his common sense.

Unfortunately, he couldn't fuck her yet. If he did, all his well-laid plans would be ruined.

She wasn't ready. Not emotionally, anyway. When he did make love to Amy, he wanted her to wake up the next morning without one iota of regret. He wanted her to know it was the best step she could have taken. Yes, she might want to fuck him tonight, but by tomorrow morning she'd be appalled. She'd wake up comparing him to Simon and her father and every other man who had walked out of her life.

There was no question about it. She wasn't ready, although ever so slowly, she was getting there—and he couldn't deny he enjoyed tormenting her just a little in the process. His encounter with Lexi may have been unplanned, but it turned into a perfect excuse to torment Amy a little more, stir up her awareness of him.

He bent his knee back and forth a couple of times. A little

tender perhaps, but nothing serious. Then he rolled his shoulders. After Amy's massage and his bath, they should feel loose and relaxed. They didn't. They were as tightly wound up as the rest of him. Lexi's cricket bat might not have caused much damage, but the memory of Amy's touch made him ache.

Damn. Lexi's cricket bat. She'd attacked him with a frigging lethal weapon. Heck, she'd hit out with such force, he'd still be unconscious if the bat had met its target: the back of his head.

To say he'd been pissed off with his sister was an understatement, but Lexi had redeemed herself. She'd obviously done a great job on Amy. Her call must have been pretty convincing. Amy may have teased him, but she couldn't hide the fear or the anxiety in her eyes. She'd been more than a little concerned about him.

He'd phone Lexi first thing in the morning to say thank you.

When at last he felt ready to do up his pants, he headed into the lounge and suppressed a smile when he saw the towel neatly folded on a chair. He'd toyed with her enough for now. For the rest of the night he'd keep their relationship platonic. He'd be so damn platonic he'd make a priest look like a porn star.

"Whatcha watching?"

"Not much. Just seeing what's on."

Was it his imagination or was she deliberately not looking at him? "Anything interesting?" He helped himself to some more food and sat next to her on the couch.

"Not really." Definitely avoiding eye contact. There was that strained quality to her voice too.

"Want some sushi?"

"No, thanks. Had enough." Did she squirm?

Jess Dee

"So..." He was determined to get her to relax again. "How's work going?" Her shoulders were so tight he could practically see knots forming.

"Not bad." She studiously kept her eyes on the TV.

Getting her to relax was harder than he thought. Amy was embarrassed. A reddish blush stained her cheeks. "Been busy?"

For a couple of moments she looked indecisive. Her eyes darted to the front door and back as she gnawed on her lower lip. "Very. For some reason we've had a rush of new patients and there's hardly been time to breathe."

"Anything interesting?"

She took a deep breath and turned to face him. Resolve steeled her expression. She was going to play this cool. "One case. They're not my patients, though. Maggie referred them to one of the other counselors. I'm just too busy."

Daniel watched her play nervously with a lock of hair. She wound it around her finger, tugged it down and let it loose, then wound it around her finger again. "Tell me about them."

"They're a professional couple with an unusual request."

"They want to get a child genetically cloned?"

"Not quite." Amy laughed. It was a tense laugh, but a laugh nevertheless. "They want to have a baby but can't do it alone."

"Why not?"

"They're both women."

"That would make it a bit difficult," Daniel agreed with a smile. "Have you had gay couples in before?"

"A few. They get a bit tricky because of the legal and social ramifications."

"Like what?"

"Like who'll carry the baby and what rights does the other

116

partner have? Are they going to use a known or an anonymous sperm donor?" Her voice became animated, like it always did when she spoke about her work. "Will the donor take on any paternal duties? Is he HIV free? It can, and usually does, get rather complicated."

"Isn't there any way of simplifying it?"

"Well, they could do it themselves with a willing and known donor. Success rates are much lower though. Then there's still all the parenting issues."

"How will they decide?"

"Through a lot of counseling and information."

"Wish you were seeing them?" Amy would have loved the challenge. She was that sort of person.

For the first time since he walked back into the room, she seemed to relax. "Yeah. It's a little frustrating not being able to take on every case. The counselor they're using is good and if there are any problems, she'll ask for assistance." She changed the subject. "What about you? Ready for tomorrow?"

"Sure am." Although job offers had poured in after his exhibition, he rejected them all and took the last few weeks off. The shoot at POWS was gut-wrenching and he needed time out to regroup.

Tomorrow he was starting work again. A woman's glossy had asked him to do a fashion shoot. He anticipated a week there would be a good entrance back into the field.

"I'll miss the sleep-ins and surfing though, 'specially now that the weather's a bit warmer. Did I tell you what the shoot is?" he asked. "It's the Oz Designers' Spring Collection. I'll be completely in the know about the upcoming fashions. Ask me anything you want to know about dressing for sunshine." He paused then said with authority, "I've been told orange is the new black." He was told no such thing, but at least his

117

comment had the desired effect. Amy laughed.

"What about skirt length?" she asked. "Mini, midi or long?"

He looked at her and shook his head. "Skirts are so last year, daahling. Anyone who's anyone in the industry knows that. The best dressed people are wearing pants this spring." He waited a second then added, "Orange pants."

Amy snorted. "Lucky you're filming the models and not dressing them."

A couple of months ago she would have made some comment about undressing them as well. It was way too good an opportunity to miss. She would have procured great joy from taking the piss out of him. A couple of months ago she'd have been right. There would've been a lot of undressing of models going on.

But not anymore.

"How are you feeling? Has the time off work helped you?"

Daniel smiled to himself. She couldn't hide that side of her—Amy the caregiver, the nurturer. No matter what he'd put her through, she still worried about him and the effect being at the hospital had on him.

If it were anyone else, he would have brushed off the question and changed the topic. "A little," he answered honestly. "For a while there, I couldn't distance myself from some of the kids. I identified too strongly with them. It hurt." It still did. His stomach twisted every time he thought of the ward.

"I guess whenever you were in a room with one of them you relived the times you sat with your sister while she was sick." Her voice was gentle, yet probing.

"I did. Especially with Vicky. She reminded me so much of Sarah."

"How?" Her eyes remained trained on his face.

"Her attitude to her illness. She was so positive the whole time. She knows there's a chance she could—" his voice cracked and he swallowed, "—she could die. Yet she was so brave and so funny. She never gave up hope, even when she was so sick she couldn't talk without throwing up." A muscle twitched in his jaw.

"She has a younger brother, Theodore. She worries about him and what he's going through. Every time she mentioned him, I thought about Sarah. Sarah always asked how Lex and I were doing. She worried about us even though she was the one going through the treatment." He closed his eyes and shook his head as painful memories poured through. "I thought about the days when she felt so bad she didn't even want to see us. And—" he paused and frowned, "—and then I remembered how rejected I felt. Christ, how selfish is that? Sarah was sick and I sat there feeling rejected?"

"Oh Danny." Amy grabbed his hand. "You were a child. A scared, anxious child."

"I was a demanding brat. I insisted my parents pay us as much attention as they gave Sarah and then got pissed off when they didn't. I didn't understand at the time that they couldn't." Hell, he hadn't expected to reveal any of this. Yet the need to get it all off his chest was overwhelming. He had to talk to someone and who better than Amy?

"You were twelve." Her voice was so soft, so understanding. "How could you possibly appreciate all the dynamics that were going on? All you knew was that your sister was sick and your parents were focused more on her than on either you or Lexi. Add to that your own feelings about Sarah's illness. It's a lot for a boy to cope with."

"Sometimes," Daniel admitted, surprised by his own candidness, "I didn't try to cope with it at all. I just pretended nothing was wrong. I'd go to school and live this fantasy where everyone was healthy. The days were much easier that way. I even remembered how to laugh again. Then I'd get home and find Mum crying, or my aunt waiting to watch us while my parents were at the hospital, and just as quickly I remembered there was nothing normal about our family after all."

"I bet that made you feel guilty, trying to live a normal life when Sarah's life was anything but."

Daniel was stunned. That's exactly how he felt. Guilty. He just hadn't understood it then. He'd berate himself over his audacity to be happy. Then fly into a rage because he didn't know how to deal with his self-recriminations. "I wasn't an easy child to live with during that time."

"Oh, Danny." She squeezed his hand. "You were trying to be normal, to find some sanity in an abnormal situation. That's human nature. It's called self-preservation. It would have been far more worrying if you hadn't tried to make the best of the situation."

He smiled at her. "Both Sarah and Vicky said the same thing. No matter how bad it got, they had to make the best of a bad situation." It was only when Vicky had said it to him that he realized she was right. It was then he resolved to make the most of his situation with Amy.

"Wise words from wise children," Amy said. "How are you feeling, now that you've had time to put a little space between yourself and the hospital?"

"A little more resolved, I guess. Kids do get sick and some don't survive. Hell, I don't like it, but I've learned to accept it."

She was silent for a while. He could practically see the cogs turning in her mind before she asked quietly, "What if Vicky died? How would you feel then?"

Shit, that is a tough one. How would he feel? "Devastated," he said at last. "But at least I'd be able to distance myself from her death. Before my stint at the ward, I wouldn't have been able to separate my feelings for her from my feelings for Sarah. Now I can."

Amy shifted so her whole body faced him. She pulled her knees up onto the couch, pressing against his thigh. Her entire focus was on the conversation and she seemed unaware that she was touching him. Although he was conscious of it, this time the contact was not arousing. It was comforting.

"Your fear of losing Sarah must have been overwhelming."

"It was. For a long time I'd forgotten that. The elation that came with her remission buried my fears. It was so much easier to focus on the happy than the sad, so I didn't try to remember what might have happened."

"That's pretty much how you live your life now, isn't it? Focusing on the happy, not the sad. That's why you always look at the positive side of life."

Daniel nodded. "I guess so."

"But you weren't left completely unscathed were you?"

"What are you talking about?"

Amy gnawed on her lower lip and held his hand in both of hers. "I think your fear of Sarah's possible death scarred you in another aspect of your life."

He shook his head, unsure of what she was getting at.

"I think," she said gently, "your fear of losing Sarah has translated into your relationships with women. Your reluctance to commit to anyone—to get involved in a serious relationship—stems from your fear of losing someone special in your life."

Daniel digested her words in silence.

"The fact that Sarah survived gave you the courage to be with a woman. But the knowledge that someone so close to you almost died made you scared another person you care deeply about might die. It's easier not to care at all. To cut your relationships off before they become meaningful."

His natural instinct was to deny it. *No. I've never had a meaningful relationship with another woman because I'm in love with you.* But after letting the idea sink in, he decided that maybe she wasn't so far off course. He hadn't committed to a long-term relationship, *ever.* Not even with Amy. He'd never even tried to get involved with her until now. The shoot had changed him. He was finally ready to take that step.

He was startled at her insightfulness. "You know what, Morgan? It never occurred to me my fear of Sarah dying may have affected me in other ways." He wanted to tell her he was ready for a commitment, as long as it was with her. But *she* wasn't ready to hear it. "You've given me a lot to think about."

He paused, choosing his words carefully. "It's only fair to give you something to think about as well."

She looked startled and tried to let go of his hand. Not ready to break contact yet, he held tight.

"I'll make you a deal, Morgan. I promise to look at my fear of commitment in a different light..."

"If...?"

He waited a heartbeat and looked her in the eyes as he said, "If you try to look at me in a different light."

Chapter Nine

It wasn't her usual practice to visit clients in hospital, but for Mary Stevens she made an exception. The woman had been a patient at the clinic for over five years and Amy knew her well. Knew the incredible lengths Mary had gone to in order to fall pregnant and then the heartbreaking agony she experienced with each failed attempt. She therefore had a pretty good idea how Mary felt after the birth of her very healthy baby boy. For this one time, it was appropriate to visit the hospital.

Besides, it would do her the world of good to move away from the chaos of her disordered thoughts about Daniel to the chaos of the maternity ward, where Mary lay, happy, content and tired.

Amy was just plain tired. Tired of wondering what the hell to do about Daniel. Of dreaming and fantasizing about him. Of wanting him and not wanting to want him. What a messed up, bitch of a situation. She wished they could go back to what they were before. Friends. Just plain old friends.

She wasn't particularly thrilled by his request that she look at him in a different light. She'd been doing her best to switch that damn light off. There were suddenly too many unexpected dynamics happening in their friendship. Too many physical interactions. Whenever they touched of late, no matter how meaningless the gesture, sparks flared between them. The usual jokes and teasing were now supercharged with sexual tension. The very air between them seemed to shimmer with unspoken lust and desire.

Lust and desire did not fare well with platonic friendship. Perhaps if Daniel had mentioned a shift in his emotions, or made her feel she was somehow different from the women he usually dated, she would be less reluctant to become involved with him. But truthfully, she did not believe he could separate her from his long string of lovers.

She couldn't help but remember his words on the Coogee promenade, when she'd tried to rationalize away their behavior at his exhibition. Couldn't forget the laughter in his eyes, or the impish grin that teased her as he'd asked, *Are you saying you want a long-term commitment from me?* As if the very idea were hilarious.

It was. To Daniel. He was incapable of commitment. There was no doubt in her mind that if they became lovers, even their friendship would not be enough to keep him by her side. He would eventually leave her like he left the rest.

Was she willing to take the risk? No way.

It's what made her situation so unbearable. While she wasn't prepared to become his lover, sleeping with him was practically the only thing she thought about. Night after night, awake or asleep, she'd lie in bed dreaming about him. Images of him consumed her. Dressed, naked, just wearing a towel, kissing her mouth, kissing her breasts, kissing her intimately. Making love to her.

Wherever she went she saw him. She mistook complete strangers for her best friend. As soon as she blinked and her vision cleared, she realized she was being foolish. But it was how she lived at the moment. In a state of perpetual arousal, her body a voracious pit of desire.

She didn't want their relationship to change. Didn't want the added complication of sex. All she wanted was the same old friendship they always had. Period.

Amy closed the door to Mary's room and left the maternity ward. She yawned. The situation between her and Daniel was all messed up. She was losing sleep over the man. What she really needed right now was a good dose of caffeine. It was only noon and she still had the rest of the day to get through.

As she walked into the hospital coffee shop, she cursed herself for tumbling into another one of her daydreams. Sitting at a table, innocently drinking a coke, was none other than the cause of all her grief.

However, no matter how many times she blinked, Daniel's features did not change. It took her a good couple of seconds to realize she was staring at the real thing and not some conjured vision of him.

"Danny?"

He looked up and his eyes flashed with surprise a heartbeat before a very wicked smile spread across his face. "Hey, babe."

Uh oh. She'd seen that smile before. Alarm bells shrieked in her head as he stood, his eyes gleaming with intent.

"What are you doing here?"

"Visiting." His voice was low and seductive. The bells rang louder. "Come here. Let me say a proper hello." Right there in the middle of the hospital canteen, he took her hand, pulled her close and kissed her.

What the hell was he doing? Had he completely lost his mind? Oh God, did it even matter? Amy simply melted, her body liquefying right there. Chaste as his kiss was, his lips were warm and sexy and held a hint of a million forbidden fantasies. In the space of a couple of seconds, she identified every single

125

one of them.

Daniel pulled away and it was over. She was weak at the knees and craved more.

Holy crap. What was it about Daniel and kissing her in public? He was developing a bit of a thing for it. Never mind public places, what was he doing kissing her, period? She agreed to *think* about him differently, not *act* differently towards him.

Her temper started to simmer. Of all the inappropriate places for him to try his luck. For God's sake, they were in a *hospital.* "Just what the hell—?"

He cut her off with his mouth, kissing her again until the last drop of anger drained from her body and she clutched him helplessly. His taste lingered on her tongue when he withdrew his head and Amy realized it had become familiar. Too familiar. Friends shouldn't recognize each other's flavor. Then again, his mouth wasn't the only taste she was familiar with, was it?

Bottom line, she had sampled several parts of Daniel and each one was better than the last. She'd never forget the tang of his desire for her, not when she'd relished every last drop. She licked her lips as the salty memory of Daniel's come filled her mouth, replacing the sweetness of the Coke he'd been drinking.

A soft, strangled groan came from Daniel. "Christ, babe." His voice was hoarse. "Are you trying to give me a heart attack?"

She poked her finger at his chest. "You kissed me."

"Yeah, but that look in your eyes. You're just begging to be—"

"Daniel?"

A voice from the table where Daniel sat broke into their conversation. They both turned to stare.

Leona Ramsey looked a little pissed off. "Hello? I thought you were having coffee with me?"

So that explained Daniel's irrational behavior. Amy could almost hear the pieces of the puzzle clicking into place. Leona was Daniel's married admirer. He was continuing their charade from the beach. No wonder he kissed her.

"Sorry 'bout that." Daniel smiled. He didn't appear the least bit apologetic. "Here, let me introduce the two of you." He held Amy's hand and said, "Amy, this is Leona Ramsey, a pediatrician from POWS. Leona, this is Amy Morgan, my...friend."

Amy struggled to regain her composure.

It wasn't easy. First of all, she was hot and bothered. Second, Daniel was hard and bothered. Third, Leona Ramsey was having a drink with Daniel, and that was just plain bothersome. Amy hadn't even noticed her sitting there. Not surprising considering she'd developed tunnel vision around Daniel. He was the only thing she ever saw nowadays. Real or imagined.

Daniel squeezed her hand, and she belatedly realized she eyed the doctor with distaste. She pasted a smile on her face. "Forgive me, I never saw you there. It's nice to meet you."

Leona stared daggers at her. "Yes, I'm sure."

Silent tension simmered between the two women. "Leona was just telling me about the ward," Daniel said. "All the renovations are finished and it looks pretty good. I'm on my way up there." He looked at Amy. "Why don't you join me? Come and see what they've done."

She hesitated. A quick glance at her wrist watch told her she really needed to get back to her office, but at the same time she wanted to see the ward.

"Vicky's back in hospital," he said quietly. "I was going to drop in and give her a little gift. Would you like to meet her?"

The pained look in Daniel's eyes as he conveyed that bit of information helped her decide. "I'd love to."

"I have patients to see so I'll head up with you," Leona said. Not entirely sure whether this was true, Amy suspected Leona used it as an excuse to spend more time with Daniel.

Odd woman. Perhaps someone should explain to her that subtlety was a far bigger turn on for her friend than the obvious advances she made? Daniel wasn't interested. Couldn't she see that? It was so glaringly obvious. If she *had* been Daniel's girlfriend, she would've happily spelled it out for Leona.

But she wasn't. So she kept her mouth shut.

The three of them caught a lift up to the eighth floor and walked across a long, narrow corridor to POWS. Amy was struck by Daniel's easy, sexy stride and she suppressed a grin. "You're not limping anymore. Your knee must be improving."

Daniel had the grace to squirm before he shrugged and said, "It twinges every now and again, but it feels fine. No thanks to my sister."

"And your shoulder?"

"A bit tender still."

Amy resisted the urge to shake her head and laugh. She could attach a microscope to his knee and shoulder, study them intensely for three solid days and still not see any sign of bruising. Daniel was just a big baby.

With a very adult body.

Oh God. Don't go there.

Leona pushed open a pair of swinging doors and they walked inside. "I have patients to see." She nodded curtly at Amy and gave Daniel a slow once over before walking off.

They shared a little smile as they watched the doctor stalk

away.

"You could have warned me." Amy laughed, both relieved and disappointed that Daniel's kisses had been nothing more than a ruse. "I didn't know what the hell you were doing."

"There wasn't time to explain. I had to act. I was on my way to the ward when Leona blindsided me. I didn't want to be rude, so I agreed to have a drink with her. I can't begin to tell you how *extremely* happy I was to see you. You saved me from another grueling invitation over to her place."

"Glad I could help." Was she? In essence, Daniel had kissed her. Again. And once again she was left aroused and hungry for more.

"Me too." He grinned. "What are you doing here?"

"I came to see a client."

"Everything okay there?"

"Better than okay. She just had a baby."

"Congratulations. Must be nice to reap the rewards of your work, I'm sure."

"As it must be for you." She stared over his shoulder. "The ward is charming."

Daniel looked around, his face absorbed and curious. He shook his head and a huge grin spread over his face. "This place looks incredible."

She could only agree. Although she'd never been in the ward before, Daniel's exhibition had given her a good idea of how it had been. Run down with old wallpaper peeling off the walls, its designs faded and dull.

Now the passages gleamed with fresh paint and bright wallpaper. If one had to be in a children's hospital, this was a good one to be in.

"Look in there." Daniel headed to an alcove filled with toys and books. "They've replaced all the old junk. Everything's new and unused." He was like a small kid and she suspected more excited about the changes than most of the children.

He should be. He was the one responsible for them.

They stopped at the nurses' station. New filing cabinets lined the walls while boxes from recently unpacked computers lay on the floor, waiting to be discarded. Not only was the ward more presentable, it also had a lot more modern technology, making administration easier.

Amy recognized a few of the nursing staff from Lexi's party and from the exhibition, and she and Daniel chatted with them a while, until Daniel asked for Vicky's room number. She sensed a little apprehension in his gait as they made their way to her room.

"Maybe I should stay outside while you go in." She was reluctant to invade the little girl's privacy.

"No. I've told Vicky all about you. I'm sure she'll want to meet you."

Why would he have told Vicky about her? There wasn't time to ask. Daniel had stepped up to a closed door and knocked softly before sticking his head inside.

"Hi there. Feeling up to visitors?" She didn't hear a response but Daniel opened the door wider and motioned for her to walk inside with him.

A quick glance revealed a cozy, inviting room, the walls done in the same colors as the corridors. The bed was made up with crisp linen in soft pastel shades of orange, lime and lemon. There were two armchairs covered in matching fabric and a bookshelf sat against the far wall, overflowing with books and toys. A TV and DVD player hung suspended from the ceiling.

The only difficult thing to take in was the slip of a girl lying in the bed. She was so tiny that at first look, Amy would have estimated her age to be around seven or eight had she not known Vicky was ten. Her hair looked as though it had been shaved off and was only just beginning to grow back. The wonders of chemotherapy.

"Hey, slugger," Daniel said affectionately. "I thought they sent you home weeks ago."

"They did," a small voice responded. "But then they brought me back." Vicky laughed weakly. "I guess they like me too much to let me go."

Amy's chest tightened and she blinked back her tears.

"Nah," Daniel said, "I think they just wanted a professional opinion on the wallpaper."

"It's nice." She looked at Amy. "Who's your friend?"

Amy walked forward. "My name's Amy." She held her hand out.

Vicky took it in hers and gave it a firm shake, firmer than Amy expected. "You don't have to be scared, you know," she told Amy. "I'm sick, but I won't break." Wise eyes, so out of place on the face of a girl so young, seemed to probe and then she said, "You're Daniel's girlfriend."

Amy smiled. She couldn't help but like the girl. "I'm Daniel's best friend. I've known him since high school."

"I have a best friend too, but he doesn't come visit me here. His mum won't let him."

"That must upset you."

"Kind of. But I understand. It's frightening for him to come into a hospital where there are very sick children." She looked solemnly at Amy.

"You understand a lot for someone so young."

Vicky shrugged. "It's taken a while to get it. At first I was hurt coz I thought he didn't like me anymore. But now I

131

understand it's just the cancer he doesn't like. He doesn't know how to deal with it. Neither does his mum. That's why she won't let him come see me."

"You must miss him."

"I did. We speak a lot on the phone now and he tells me what's going on at school. He promised to come visit as soon as I get out of hospital this time. And," she turned to Daniel, "he's going to bring all the Harry Potter DVDs so we can watch them together."

"Cool!" Daniel said with enthusiasm. "Did you finish the fourth book?"

"Yep." Vicky looked at Amy to explain. "Daniel gave me the first five Harry Potter books. I started reading them in hospital and when I felt too sick to read myself, Daniel read to me."

"So, what did you think?"

"I *loved* number four. And number five."

"You read that one too?" Daniel was clearly impressed.

Vicky nodded. "When I got home. Theodore and I read it together. Theodore's my little brother," she told Amy.

Amy nodded. Daniel had told her about Theodore. "Did he like the books?"

"Very much, although he was a little young to understand it all. I had to explain a lot of it to him." Amy imagined Vicky had explained a lot of things to her little brother, and not just about Harry Potter.

"Well then," Daniel said, "I guess I'm just in time."

"For what?" Vicky's eyes grew large.

"To give you this." He handed her a wrapped parcel.

She pushed herself up slowly. Amy saw how much effort it cost her. But the child's smile was enormous. A touch of pink shaded her pale cheeks.

"I know what it is," she exclaimed before she'd even opened the present. "And it's perfect. Thank you."

Little fingers worked at the sticky tape until she had the paper off. She held it up and grinned in delight. "It's the sixth book."

"Let me know when you're done with it. There's the seventh one too. The last in the series." Daniel's smile was just as large.

Amy stared at her friend, her heart filled with silly warm fuzzies. Daniel honestly was a sweetheart. Without a doubt the nicest man she knew.

Vicky nodded. "You've got a deal. I just know Theo will love this too." She changed the subject. "Last time I saw you, you told me I encouraged you to do something. Have you done it?" She smiled at him and winked, scrunching up the right side of her face.

Daniel smiled back. "I'm in the middle of it."

Amy listened with interest.

"Is it working?"

"Too early to tell. I've made some progress though."

Vicky looked at Amy then back at Daniel. "You won't give up, will you?"

"And let you down? Not a chance."

"Well, let me know how it works out, okay?"

"Okay," Daniel agreed. "Now we'd better let you get some rest."

The dark circles under Vicky's eyes stood out on her abnormally white skin. "I think I need it," she admitted.

"I'll be in soon to see you again."

And no doubt drop off another gift. Amy smiled at the thought. "Nice meeting you, Vicky. Hope you feel better."

"See you soon, slugger. Bye."

"Bye Amy. Bye Daniel, and remember...don't give up."

He winked at her and then they left the room.

Daniel led her to the doctors' room, where he sagged into a chair with a heavy sigh. He rubbed a hand over his eyes. "Damn, she looks awful. Worse than she did in the middle of her chemotherapy."

"She adores you. Her face lit up when she saw you."

"Yeah, well I'm pretty crazy about her too. It's amazing how much she taught me about life."

"She's learned a lot in her short one." Amy regarded Daniel thoughtfully. "What was that whole conversation about? What did Vicky inspire you to do?"

He looked at her, his eyebrow arched. "You don't know?"

"How could I? You were both so cryptic in there I didn't know what you were talking about." Nevertheless, her heart began to pound.

Daniel stared at her, his blue eyes bright with intensity. "It's all about you."

"Me?" She swallowed. "You discussed me with Vicky?"

He smiled a mysterious, sexy smile. "We both spoke about the important things in our lives."

"So what are they?" A memory intruded just then, of the two of them sitting at Tamarama the day after he finished his shoot. What were the words he had used then?

Vicky forced me to look at my life and my behavior quite thoroughly. I'm just not happy with where I am right now.

It was all connected. Whatever he was about to tell her, it was exactly the thing he felt he wasn't ready to discuss back then. And it was about her. What on earth could it be?

"Danny? What did you say about me?" Her heart drummed unsteadily.

The door opened and Leona walked into the office. She looked at them in surprise. "You're still here? I thought you'd be gone by now."

Amy nearly moaned out loud. Leona's timing couldn't have been worse.

"I'm glad you haven't left yet." She looked coquettishly at Daniel, oblivious to Amy's turmoil. "I wanted to discuss tonight with you. I thought we could get together."

Amy shook her head in disbelief. Was the woman stupid? Leona had seen Daniel kissing her at least twice now and still she could not take a hint. Apart from that, Daniel looked harassed. He'd just seen Vicky and was upset by her appearance. The last thing he needed was Leona bugging him.

To top it all, the good doctor had interrupted a very private, very pivotal, moment.

She checked her watch. Time was running out. She had an appointment with a client in less than half an hour. Daniel wasn't going to get a chance to tell her his big secret.

Damn the woman.

Enough was enough. "Look Leona," she interjected before Daniel could say anything. "Daniel has plans tonight—with me." Actually, he didn't, but Leona didn't need to know that. "So no, I don't think you'll be getting together with him. Not tonight, nor any night soon. Get it?" She turned to Daniel and softened her tone. "My place, around seven?"

Daniel nodded. His dimples flashed as he tried to hide a grin. "Don't forget, I'm cooking tonight."

Aware of a glowering Leona standing beside her, Amy gave him a slow smile. "You sure were last night." After giving it a second thought, she planted a sultry kiss on his lips.

His eyes closed and he murmured a low, "Mmm..."

The sound reverberated from her breasts down to her belly and lower. She had to clear her throat before she could speak. "I have to go back to work. See you later." With a casual wave at Leona, she walked out the room.

Daniel watched Amy leave with a barely repressed smile. His misery over seeing Vicky in such a bad state was temporarily masked. What a stroke of luck running into Amy like that. God, if he'd have thought about it before, he'd have choreographed the whole damn thing himself. He laughed out loud, grabbed Leona and twirled her around.

"Put me down, you stupid lug." She was chuckling by the time Daniel set her back on her feet.

"Thank you," he said. "You were fantastic. I can't believe how quickly you fell into character. I hadn't even introduced you to Amy and already you were playing the hard-nosed bitch."

"Beside the fact that I recognized her from the party, the look of undisguised adulation on your face was a dead giveaway. There was no question about who she was."

Daniel shrugged. "What can I say? I'm a man possessed."

Leona laughed. "Say you'll never subject me to such nonsense again."

"I can't promise that. You do it so well. So did Amy. It took a while, but when she realized who you were, she really played her part, don't you think?"

Leona looked thoughtful for a moment. "Amy wasn't playing. She took those kisses very seriously."

"You think so?"

"I'm well qualified to know how a woman responds when

136

she's enjoying a kiss," Leona said. "Amy enjoyed those kisses."

Daniel felt exuberant. "You know what, Leona? I think deep down in there, there is a woman with a big heart and a soft spot for romance."

"I have no problem with romance. I'm just choosy about who I get to be romantic with."

"Man, that's no lie." When Daniel met Leona a few years back, he found her aloofness towards him quite refreshing. He'd made a move and she turned him down cold.

"You weren't my type," Leona reminded him with a smile.

Daniel laughed. "Yeah. I was pretty embarrassed when I found out."

"But your advances were flattering."

"Your rejection wasn't." He attempted a frown but grinned instead.

"Are you really cooking Amy dinner tonight? Or was that just for show?"

Daniel sighed. "Just for show. Trust me, the next time I cook her dinner, I'll be making her breakfast the next morning too."

Leona looked at him, her round eyes filled with compassion. "Oh, you poor man. It's such a pity your self-confidence is so low. It must be your lack of experience with women."

Daniel gave Leona a halfhearted smile. His only lack of experience was with Amy and it was just about killing him.

"I wouldn't worry," Leona reassured him. "I have a strong suspicion all that is about to change."

ℰↄ

Back at work, Amy drummed her nails restlessly on her desk as her mind raced. When she could bear it no more, she swore out loud and grabbed the phone.

"What did Vicky inspire you to tell me," she demanded as soon as Daniel answered.

She heard him chuckle on the other side. "Eating away at you, is it?"

"I thought you were feeling miserable after your visit to the hospital," she snapped, irritated that he sounded so relaxed when curiosity gnawed at her.

His tone remained upbeat. "I *was* miserable after seeing Vicky. But it's hard to stay like that when I know she and all the other kids are so comfortable in their newly refurbished ward."

"Oh..." She should have felt bad about snapping at him, but she didn't. She was too focused on her objective. "So what did you want to tell me?"

"That I'm making dinner for you tonight, at your place? How does pasta sound?"

She could practically see the gleam in his eyes. "You're not invited, you know that. Besides, you can't cook."

"I thought you told Leona I was cooking last night?"

"Look, stop changing the subject. You know that whole act was for Leona's benefit."

"Was it?" His voice drifted over the phone like a low, sensual hum. "Your kiss didn't seem like an act at all."

She froze for a second and then resumed her agitated finger tapping. That kiss wasn't an act. Yes, she used Leona as an excuse, but that's all Leona was. An excuse. She kissed Daniel because she wanted to. Electric fencing between the two of them couldn't have stopped her.

Unsure how to respond, she chose to ignore his words. "What were you and Vicky talking about?"

His sigh was her answer.

"Please, Danny. Can you please just lay it on the line for me?"

There was a moment's hesitation before he said, "Not over the phone. Why don't you come round tomorrow? I'll be home late in the afternoon. We can talk then."

Chapter Ten

It was late afternoon the next day and Amy stood in Daniel's apartment, determined to get him to talk. Thanks to her friend, she had suffered yet another sleepless night. What the hell was he so secretive about? What had he discussed with Vicky? More importantly, what did it have to do with her?

Even if she had to use a crowbar to pry open his mouth, she would get it out of him. If it was the last thing he ever did, he'd speak to her.

Despite her overwhelming need to find out his secret, she needed a swim first. It had been an abnormally hot day for spring and the approaching sunset brought no relief. The meteorological bureau had reported a record high and Amy was sweltering. The weather and her agitation about Daniel combined to raise her own body temperature a good fifty degrees or so.

Hot and flushed, she slipped on her swimsuit in the bathroom. She was too tense and sweaty to have a meaningful conversation with him right now. There was a pool at the back of his building and she was determined to go and calm herself in its cool water.

She looked at her reflection in the mirror, eyeing the tiny black bikini she wore. Why had she chosen this particular suit? It was so flimsy it barely covered the essential bits. Why hadn't she brought her sensible one piece? The answer, of course, was Daniel.

Something changed inside her yesterday, like a cog clicking into place. It probably happened while she watched Daniel with Vicky. Something in her heart melted when she saw the way he acted towards the young girl.

He treated her like an adult, showing her absolute respect, yet handled her with such gentleness, affection and care. The girl was crazy about him. Amy couldn't blame him. She was crazy about him herself.

Daniel was just plain nice. The nicest man she ever knew. The sexiest man she ever knew.

She was fed up pretending she wasn't attracted to him. She was. In a big way. At some point soon she was going to give in and admit it to Daniel. Her tiny scrap of a bikini was just the beginning. Just a tiny hint of her feelings.

Daniel sat on a couch, browsing through a photography magazine. He wore a pair of navy swimming shorts that rode low on his hips. They looked good on him. They'd probably look better packed away in a drawer somewhere, and not interfering with the smooth lines of his body.

She mentally shook her head. "I'm ready."

He looked up and gave her a very slow once-over. "Nice suit." His voice was unexpectedly mild.

"Thank you." She gave him a bland smile, hiding her disappointment. He'd had a long enough look. Didn't he approve?

With a wide and not-so-innocent smile, he added, "I think my five-year-old niece has one just like it."

Typical.

"It's about the same size too."

Amy studied her nails, doing her best to ignore him and the sudden flame shooting through her stomach. How did he do it? Insult her and get her all hot at the same time?

"But," he continued, unfazed by her apparent disinterest, "Michelle has a little problem with her bikini. Every time she jumps in the pool, her top slips off."

She rolled her eyes. "Isn't it lucky I have something to hold my top in place."

"You sure do." His gaze trained on her breasts. Blue eyes shone with pure male interest.

"I was talking about the strap," she snapped. Inordinately pleased to feel his gaze on her nipples, she knew he could see them beading. For once she did nothing to hide her response to him.

Let him stew over that one.

"Oh, yeah. Sure. Me too."

If he thought interesting things were happening to the top half of her body, what would his reaction be if he discovered what was going on in the lower half? The sweet tugs of desire between her legs had her groin crying out for the same attention he gave her breasts. She toyed with the idea of stripping off her miniscule bikini, which felt more constrictive than a corset. But true to form, common sense got the better of her. Until Daniel told her what he and Vicky had been discussing, he wasn't getting any of her.

But after that, well...who knew?

She stalked to the door and yanked it open. "I'm going for a swim. Care to join me?"

"Of course." His voice was deceptively innocent. "Someone has to make sure your top stays in place." He fell in step beside her, singing softly to himself.

Amy glowered at him when she heard the lyrics.

"*She wore an itsy-bitsy, teeny-weeny...*" She punched his arm before he could finish.

Just as they reached the pool, a man and two young children were leaving. The place was deserted. Daniel dropped his towel and dived in. She made out the words, "*Yellow, polka-dot bikini...*" just before he hit the water.

Her hands on her waist, she glared at him as he began to swim lengths of the pool. There appeared to be an awful lot of effort going into his strokes. Way more than necessary. Powerful arms sliced through the water as broad shoulders skimmed the surface. Long, toned legs and forceful kicks sent him racing as muscles rippled beneath his skin.

Amy swallowed, forgetting to be annoyed. He was magnificent. She couldn't take her eyes off him. *Bugger.* She was hot, bothered and wet, and it had nothing to do with the stream of water that hit her when Daniel dived in.

He was doing funny things to her insides. Her stomach flip-flopped and her breasts swelled in the useless restraint of her bikini top. Daniel was right. The scrap of cloth didn't offer much cover. Her taut nipples threatened to pop right out if she became any more aroused.

She dived in and swam the length of the pool underwater. When she surfaced in the deep end, Daniel was waiting for her, his arm hooked over the side of the pool. They were so close they almost touched. The urge to press up against him was strong. Every nerve ending stood at attention, utterly aware of his proximity.

Drops of water beaded on his lashes, turning his eyes a shimmering aqua. He peered down into the water between them and furrowed his brow in mock concern. "Is your top still in place?"

"Very much so." Once again she considered slipping it off.

"Oh..." Was that regret she could hear? "Well, that's a relief, I'm sure."

"Your concern for my top is touching." Maybe if she snagged the clasp on the pool wall, the top would stick to it as she swam off.

"Hey, there were little children running around here. I'm just trying to keep things decent."

She yawned. "Danny, my friend, you're a bore."

"A bore?" An evil glint appeared in his eyes. "I'll show you boring." He pushed away from the wall.

Bikini top forgotten, Amy's jaw dropped in alarm. "No, don't you dare! Don't even—"

It was too late. Daniel was underwater. She drew in a quick mouthful of air just as he grabbed her feet and pulled her under. Automatically she pinched her nose closed before a gallon of water ran up it. He'd done that to her a thousand times and every time he caught her unprepared.

You'd think I'd learn.

Arms flailing, she broke the surface snorting and swearing, vowing to get revenge.

She flipped around to pummel him, but he'd already swum off and was a few feet away. "Prepare to suffer for that!" She dove under the water and headed straight for him.

Although Daniel was a good swimmer, she was faster. Always had been. Before long she was behind him, plowing into his back, grabbing him by the shoulders and trying to force him down. It had never been a problem when they were kids. He'd go under as soon as she pushed. But he was bigger now. Much bigger. She had no luck dunking him.

When had his shoulders filled out like that?

They reached shallow water and Daniel stood up with ease, laughing.

She clung to him, her arms wrapped around his neck and her legs around his waist, piggyback style. Darn, he felt good. Would he mind if she just rested there while she caught her breath? For the next hour or so?

His cold, wet skin rubbed against her already-aroused breasts, sending shockwaves of desire coursing through her. Each time he laughed, his body shook with mirth and vibrated against her wildly sensitive clit.

It was a good thing she wasn't thinking clearly enough to tell him a good joke. Chances of her coming the second he got the punch line were pretty high.

"It's payback time," she whispered. "And be warned...I intend to play dirty."

He twisted around to look at her. It was more luck than willpower that stopped her from coming undone at the movement.

"How dirty?"

Incapable of speech, she simply nibbled on his earlobe.

He softly moaned and encouraged as she flicked her tongue into his ear and then out again.

"That's not dirty." His voice dropped a notch. "That's below the belt."

"That's a long way from your belt." She relaxed her legs and slid down his back, torturing her breasts in the process.

He turned around. His nipples were also hard, but since the water was cold, it didn't necessarily mean anything.

She ran a finger from his knee up the inside of his shorts, lowering her voice seductively as she spoke. "Would you like to see me playing below the belt? Or would you rather I focus just here?" Reluctant to move her finger away from its current playground, she forced her hand out the water and traced the outline of his right nipple.

"You're treading on dangerous ground." His chest rumbled as he growled.

Definitely not the cold. "So, I guess it's below the belt then." A smile of smug satisfaction curving her lips, she trailed her finger down to his stomach until she touched the band of his shorts.

He inhaled sharply, his eyes dilating. *Good!* He was beginning to be affected by all of this. It was irrelevant that she was as well.

She hooked a finger under his waistband and took a step backward, tugging him along with her. He followed willingly.

"Now we're playing below the belt." She took another step and the floor dipped away. She kicked once and floated up. Daniel floated with her. Releasing her hold on his shorts, she ran her hand over the nylon fabric and down his leg.

"Amy—"

She shushed him with a finger to his lips. When she took a deep breath and ducked under water, trailing her hands past his knees to his feet, she knew she had him.

Quickly, she grasped his ankles and yanked him down.

She caught his shocked look as he went under. *Revenge is sweet.* Without waiting, she swam to the side of the pool and pulled herself out.

He surfaced, coughing and spluttering, incredulity plastered on his face. "I cannot believe you did that."

"Me neither." She grinned and picked up her towel.

"That was low."

"Yeah, you might say it was below the belt." She laughed as

she dried herself off, squeezing water from her hair. "I was good, wasn't I?"

"You don't have to be so damn smug about it."

"Now, now...let's not get bitter over this."

"You stuck your tongue in my ear."

"Yep."

"And your finger in my pants."

"You liked it."

"You tricked me."

"You were so easy."

He climbed out of the pool, muttering under his breath while Amy gloated nearby. Her revelry was short-lived. Dripping wet, he stalked up to her and glared down into her eyes. "You will regret that." He towered over her.

She already did. They were extremely close to each other and there was no water between them to dampen her awareness. A slow flush suffused her cheeks. Breathing became difficult. "Oh dear, I'm so scared," she improvised. Only it was not fear coursing through her veins. It was full-blown, red-hot desire.

"Good. Be afraid. Be very afraid." His tone was menacing.

She bit back a smile. "Please, Mister. Don't hurt little ole me."

He took a step closer. "I intend to punish you, not hurt you."

He was punishing her. His presence alone was punishment. Need pulsed through her. "Now, now. There's no need to be a sore loser." Amy dropped her towel and placed a placating hand on his chest. In an instant she regretted it—her palm burned at the contact. "Just because you lost at your own game doesn't mean you have to take your anger out on me."

147

His eyes narrowed. "I *never* lose at my own games."

Not noticing the lounger, she stepped back. It caught her behind her knees and she sat unexpectedly. A bubble of laughter escaped her. The mischievous glint returned to Daniel's eyes.

Strong, cool hands pushed against her shoulders, forcing her to lie down. She forgot to struggle against them.

"Now, if memory serves me correctly, you have a ridiculously ticklish spot just below your ribs." He held up both hands.

"No!" She threw her arms out to ward him off. "Please, no." It was too late. His fingers were on her waist and under her arms. Shrieking in protest, she pleaded with him to stop.

Relentless in his intent, he climbed on the lounger, a leg on either side of her, and tickled. She instinctively rolled into a ball, but the strategic maneuver caused problems of its own. In this position, she rubbed against wet, rock-hard legs, sending shock waves reeling through her. She didn't know which torture was worse—his tickling or his touch.

A plan of attack was necessary, but what could she do? Thump him? Jump him? "Please..." she begged instead. "I can't take it anymore."

"Are you admitting defeat?"

"Never." *I'd consider it if you'd kiss me.*

Drops of water splashed down onto her bikini top as he bent over her. His chest was so near. "Defeat?" His breath was warm on her face.

All she needed to do was arch her back and her breasts would press against him. "Uh-uh." Oh, how her nipples ached for contact.

He tickled her again, his arm brushing against the side of

her breast.

A flame ignited inside her. "Okay, okay," she relented. "I admit defeat." *Now kiss me.*

"Good. Let that be a lesson to you." He stared down at her, exultant in his conquest, his mouth an inch from hers.

"Bully." Her voice lacked conviction, the word coming out as a soft sigh.

He held her gaze for a second too long. Blood roared in her ears. *Kiss me. Now.* Nervously, she flicked her tongue out and ran it along her lower lip.

A knowing smile touched the corner of his mouth. An arrogant, sexy smile. It caught Amy in her belly and sent shivers of awareness coursing through her. Her swim had done nothing to dampen her arousal. In fact, it had the opposite effect. She was so aware of Daniel, his body and his closeness, she debated the wisdom of wrapping her legs around his waist, arching her hips and pressing herself against his cock.

He didn't give her a chance. One last wicked smile and he pushed off the lounger and stood up.

Disappointment and frustration coursed through her. Despite the heated air, she was cold. Her smile felt empty and lifeless. *Shit.* What was the point of all this fooling around? Was he just teasing her? Or was he sticking to his word and keeping their relationship platonic?

Fuck that.

She didn't want platonic. Not from him. Not anymore. The only thing she wanted was for him to get back on the lounger, lean over her again and fuck her. Hard, deep and slow. For a *very* long time.

Obviously he wasn't going to do that. She took a deep, steadying breath and got up. Much to her annoyance, her hands shook.

"Now who's the sore loser?" He stood behind her and whispered in her ear. His breath tickled her skin, sending a shiver down her spine.

Bastard. He was toying with her.

Fine. Two could play the same game. At her feet was the towel she dropped earlier. She leaned over to pick it up, deliberately keeping her legs straight, pushing her ass back in the process and pressing it into his groin.

Her mood perked up. A smirk curving her lips, she straightened and then handed him her towel. "I think you need this more than I do. Remember, there were children running around here. We have to keep things decent."

"Decent?" His smile was gone and the gleam in his eyes bordered on dangerous. Her heart began to pound. "Is that really what you want? To keep things decent?"

Hunger swept through her. Did she want to keep things decent? Good God, no. Kissing him was no longer enough. She wanted to lie down and do downright indecent things with him. Now.

It was obvious he wanted the same thing. His cock wasn't just hard, it had felt like a baseball bat nestling into her buttocks.

Her heart hammered and her breathing became labored. The time for games was over. Their relationship had reached a changing point and there was no going back. Only forward. But until she had some answers, she wasn't going anywhere.

"Daniel...?" Amy grabbed his arms, feeling tiny jolts of electricity pulsing from his skin. "That day at Tamarama, you said you'd discovered something about yourself, something you weren't ready to talk about. What was it?"

"You know what it was." His mouth was so close his breath fanned her face. "I can see it in your eyes."

She shook her head. "Spell it out for me."

"There's no need." His eyes were dark, his look heated. "You've worked it out."

"I have?"

"You have."

Her blood smoldered. The look on his face was the same glazed expression he had that day at the beach. Initially she thought he'd been worried about his situation. Now she knew better. The look on his face was desire, plain and simple. Naked desire. And it was aimed at her.

Daniel was right. She had worked it out. Finally, his secret dawned upon her. He wanted her—and had for a long time. He repeatedly told her for weeks but she refused to listen. Well, she listened now. Every cell in her body listened.

However, he couldn't have told a ten-year-old that he wanted to fuck his best friend. There had to be more to it than just desire.

"Stop screwing around, Tanner." She shook his arms as she whispered fiercely. "I think I've worked it out, but I'm not entirely sure. Clarify it for me—just so there are no misunderstandings. What exactly did you tell Vicky?"

He stared at her for the longest time, his eyes now a stormy gray. Emotion played across his face but she couldn't read it, couldn't work it out. "Daniel, please."

After a while he nodded. "I told her I don't treat you the way I should, that I take advantage of you. Of our friendship."

"And...?"

"She said I should change my behavior, my attitude. She said life's too short to mess around with the people you...care about. She told me to do whatever it took to show you how much you mean to me."

"I, uh..." Amy swallowed. Breathing became difficult. "You're my best friend. I know how much I mean to you, Dan."

"Morgan..." His whisper was seductive. "You don't have a clue."

Her heart lurched. "Then tell me." She gave his arms a weak shake. "Please, tell me."

"How specific do you want me to be?" It looked and sounded like he had difficulty breathing. His chest was so close the fine hairs sprinkled on it scraped her nipples every time he inhaled.

"Very specific." Her breasts ached from the contact.

"Then listen close, Morgan, because I'll only say it once."

When he leaned in and kissed her, she heard what he had to say. For the first time she ignored her body's response to his touch and listened to his.

He wanted her. His mouth told her as it worked hungrily on hers, teasing, licking, sucking and tasting. His arms told her as they trembled beneath her grasp. His physical reaction told her—his nipples hardened against her own tender breasts, and his hips ground into hers, pressing his erection firmly into her stomach.

Most of all, the low, throaty groan that emanated from deep inside him as he kissed her told her he wanted her. She wanted him too.

Not ready to break the kiss but knowing it was necessary, she pulled her mouth from his. "Now I know."

His eyes closed, he shook his head. "You don't know the half of it." His voice was tormented.

"Then show me." She twirled out of his arms. "Come back

to your apartment and show me everything."

Without waiting for an answer, Amy wheeled around and walked off. She reached his door and opened it without a backward glance, heading straight for the kitchen. The bottle of water she pulled out of the fridge was icy cold, unlike her. She was burning hot, engulfed by need. A fire raged inside her that even the long, cooling drink from the bottle couldn't dampen. She burned for Daniel. Wanted him with a desperation that shook her to her core. The desire to make love to him, hold him, lose herself in his kisses and make him a part of her, raged inside her like a towering inferno. She wanted to undress him and have wild, wicked sex with him.

Her breath came in short gasps and her heart slammed against her ribs. Thoughts of him, of their last hour together, echoed through her belly, reverberating in a warm heat between her legs.

The front door closed. He was there, in the apartment. Should she go to him? Should she wrap herself around his beautiful body and run her hands over his flat stomach? Relish the strength below the devastating contours of his chest? God help her, she wanted to. Wanted to strip his shorts off and render him bare and hard. In front of her, on top of her, inside her.

"Oh!" Images like that stoked the fire burning inside her. Lord, she wanted him so bad she could taste it. Taste his hot, salty skin as she kissed her way along his square jaw, taste his come as he squirted it in her mouth.

The phone rang. And rang and rang. She heard Daniel's familiar message as the machine picked up and then a blurred voice. Daniel swore before answering with a throaty hello. *Must be important.* She listened to him speak, to the low, rumbling of his voice. Images of that voice rasping in her ear, telling her of

153

his need for her, what he wanted to do to her, flashed across her mind.

Blindly she made her way out of the kitchen, clutching the cold water bottle like a lifeline. Wanton fantasies that had nothing on the real life man roared through her head.

Daniel's attention was focused on his conversation. He didn't see her hunger as she studied him. Muscles bunched in his arm as he jotted something down, carelessly shaking his wet hair as he ran his other hand through the short curls.

Amy sagged against the wall, imagining that hand running through her hair, over her back, around her waist, up to her breasts and down to her wet, pulsating core.

"How about next Tuesday?" she heard him ask.

He put the pen down, and his fingers drummed against the pad of paper, restless, disinterested. He made an impatient gesture with his hand.

Condensation beaded on the icy bottle of water she held against her chest. She rolled it from side to side, trying to cool down. The cold was a stark contrast to her feverish skin and she gasped.

He looked up—and froze.

Seconds ticked by.

"I'll call you later," he said into the phone and hung up without waiting for a reply.

Awareness hummed across the room. Daniel's Adam's apple bobbed as he swallowed. His jaw clenched as he stared at Amy in silence. The bottle dropped from her slackened hand and rolled unnoticed across the carpet.

Their eyes locked and she lifted her shaky arms behind her back and undid the straps to her top. The silence in the room was punctuated by sounds of the damp spandex dropping to the floor and then Daniel's sharp intake of breath. He did not move. Except his eyes, which had turned a familiar smoky gray. They took in every inch of her. Scorched her already burning body.

At an impossibly slow pace she nudged at her bikini bottom, inching it down her legs and kicking it aside, her gaze still locked onto his. Finally she stood before him, naked and proud.

Raw desire flashed in his eyes.

Fortune favored the bold, or so she heard, and if she wanted to get what she desired, she needed to be bold. She walked forward, her eyes never leaving his, until she stood mere inches in front of him. Trapped by his smoky gaze, she watched him touch his palm to her aroused nipple, his caress feather-light. Her breath left her throat in a hiss.

He flicked his tongue over the puckered bud of her nipple, sending sparks of excitement tingling down her spine and making her whimper.

His treatment was excruciating, his breath hot against her skin, and she shivered, almost delirious with need. She tangled her fingers in his sleek, wet curls and held his head firm, pushing her breast against his silvery-hot tongue. When it rasped over her nipple, her knees buckled.

His arms shot around her waist, catching her, supporting her. He groaned aloud and clamped his mouth over her breast, suckling her tight, tender bud, nipping, licking, teasing. Amy almost wept with longing. Moist heat pooled between her legs and oozed down her inner thighs.

She tugged his arms, urging him out of his chair, and he sensually slid his body up against hers, making every inch of her ache. He held her close, his solid chest warm against her aroused breasts.

The floor dipped away and fire shot through Amy's veins as he caught her lower lip between his teeth and nibbled gently. Heated desire took control over logic. His damp swimsuit did little to cool her feverish skin. Nor could it conceal the length of his erection pressing against her belly, driving her to the edge of sanity.

She slipped her hands under the elasticized waist and shoved the unwanted clothing down his legs. Without breaking the kiss, Daniel stepped out of his shorts. His cock, rock hard and free, poked proudly against her stomach, turning her insides to liquid.

She ran her hands around his side until they rested on his very firm, very tempting butt, then she raked her nails over the soft skin. He growled against her mouth, jerking into her.

His reaction empowered her, validated her femininity, and she ran her fingers along the hard lines of his pelvis until she brushed the satin steel of his erection. When she wrapped her hand around him, Daniel swept her up in his arms with a guttural moan and carried her to his room.

Amy's heart stuttered. As much time as she spent in his apartment, she always gave his bedroom a wide berth. There was something too intimate about that room—the place where he slept, made love to women—for her to feel comfortable there. It was a part of his world she never wanted to intrude. It was his private place.

For the first time ever, she found herself desperate to be in forbidden territory with Daniel.

He laid her down on his bed and stood before her in all his naked glory. Her mouth went dry. He was beautiful—hard, lean, hot, the epitome of masculinity and very, very aroused. The subtle scent of his spicy aftershave clung to his sheets, surrounding her. She inhaled deeply as she stared at him and her mouth began to water.

She watched him watching her, met his smoky gaze as he knelt over her. His devilish, sexy mouth parted, preparing to kiss her. Smooth, hot lips touched hers and she forgot to breathe. His tongue tortured her mouth with deep, silky strokes, stirring in her an unimaginable lust.

He braced himself on his forearms, lying above her, not quite touching yet driving her mad. Her body screamed for his embrace. She felt empty, neglected. Desperate for contact of the most intimate kind, she shoved her hips up and cried out in frustration.

He deepened his kiss in response and gradually lowered his body until finally—finally—it covered hers, enveloping her in its heat.

Greedy for more contact, her hands were everywhere, running down his sinewy back and over his firm butt. Squeezing his muscular arms, digging into his damp curls, relishing his solidity, loving his feel. Loving his response. She was so ready. The need to have all of him overwhelmed her. She bucked against him.

He dipped his hand down and groaned when he found her moist center. "Amy. Sweet, beautiful Amy. Do you have any idea what you do to me?"

Coherent speech was impossible so she settled for a long, "Oh..." as his finger found her clit and began to massage it. Pleasure rolled through her.

"Christ, babe. You're so wet." He slipped his finger in and she bore down on it.

"Please, Danny, oh..." He was doing mad things to her and although it felt good, so good, it wasn't enough.

She reached for his cock and sheathed it with her hand. "Danny?"

157

"Amy?"

"Make love to me."

A primal growl echoed through the room as Daniel stilled. His eyes closed, but not before she saw triumph and steely determination in them.

"You sure about this, babe?" he whispered.

She ground her pelvis against his hand. How much more sure could she be? "I need to feel you inside, Danny. Please, make love to me."

She adjusted her grasp as his cock grew in her palm.

When she looked up his eyes were still closed, so she bit his neck. Hard. The time for niceties was over.

His eyes flew open and locked with hers. Flames of desire burned in them.

"Now, Danny." Once again she bucked against him.

He moved his arms to either side of her face. "Say it again. Tell me what you want."

"I want you to make love to me." She twisted her waist.

"Morgan, wait!" His jaw clenched.

She stared at him uncomprehendingly. She wouldn't wait any more. Couldn't.

"I...I need a condom."

There was no way she was having anything between them. She wanted just the two of them. "I'm on the pill."

He nodded slowly. "Then we're okay." Because it was Daniel, she knew they were.

She drew her legs wider apart and gasped when the tip of his penis plunged into her. With a throaty growl and an expert thrust, he filled her.

Amy moaned in pure satisfaction. It was perfect. He was

perfect. They fit together perfectly. In awe, she opened her eyes to stare directly into Daniel's. This, them, together. It was the ultimate connection. She had never felt as close to Daniel as she did at this moment.

"Amy. Oh...Christ, Morgan..." Daniel shook his head and shuddered.

The movement reverberated through him and through his cock. Her muscles tightened convulsively around him, setting off a fresh wave of longing. She wound her legs around his waist and arched her back, frantic to get closer, take him deeper. Her hips moved, rotated in circles and then pumped up and down. Anything to get nearer to him, to get him deeper inside.

"Easy." He stilled her frenzied efforts, holding her tight, his voice agonized. Perspiration beaded on his forehead and his shoulders bunched under her touch.

When he began to move, skilled hands urged her to move with him as he rocked back and forth in an intimate and erotic rhythm. Slow at first, but gradually picking up speed. Thrust for thrust she met him, the electricity inside building each time he plunged into her.

"Amy..." His husky voice drove her wild.

The tension mounted. Vaguely she registered the soft mewling noises coming from her throat.

"Oh God, Amy." He caught her mouth with his and kissed her hard, his tongue mimicking the movement of his lower body.

It was too much. Too good. The building orgasm overwhelmed her and she let go. Wave after wave of pleasure crashed over her. As the world spun around her, she was aware of Daniel's hoarse cry as he too gave way to the exquisite release that rocked her very soul.

80

Daniel lay on the bed, cradling Amy in his arms. He felt a protectiveness deep down in his bones. She was all woman and soft curves. Tiny bumps peaked under his touch when he ran his finger down her side.

Amy had blown him away today. He'd been hard ever since she walked through the door, but when he saw her in her swimsuit, thoughts of tearing it off and covering her body with something more substantial—like himself—overrode everything else. The banter they shared did nothing to help cool his need, so he punished himself with vigorous laps in the pool, forcing away the excess energy that drummed through his veins. Then she had to go and dive in, and the cool water turned into a burning pit.

She tortured him with her cute games. Caressing him, teasing him, whipping him into a frenzy. Oh, he got his own back, tickling and tormenting her. But touching Amy was like shoving his hand into a fire. He got burned every time. Today he'd been seared all over.

He'd watched understanding dawn on her face. Seeing her eyes register his desire for her was the biggest aphrodisiac of all. However, it was when he was on the phone that she pretty much knocked his world left of center. She stared at him with those bedroom eyes and he nearly lost his mind. His knuckles turned white and went numb as he clenched the arms of the chair, fighting his instinct to pounce.

If self-control were an art, he'd be a master.

When she came to him, naked and needy, he held back and let her set the pace. That decision nearly killed him. His wildest dreams had not prepared him for the real woman. Amy was feminine and sensual and had damn near driven him over the edge. She had taken him to the ends of the universe and back and left him shattered in her wake.

His dick was flaccid for what felt like the first time in months. She had milked every last drop he had to offer. Yet, as sure as he knew he held the woman he loved, he knew it wouldn't remain soft for long. Even as he dipped his hand over the curve of her hipbone, his groin stirred.

"You asleep?" He knew she wasn't. Her breathing hadn't evened out yet and every few minutes, soft moans of contentment escaped her.

"No. Too dazed to sleep." Her voice, deep and drowsy, sent a dart of desire through him.

"Mmm...it was pretty amazing, wasn't it?"

"It...it was...wow."

He nuzzled her ear. "You were...wow. Hell, Morgan, I've waited since forever to make love to you."

She stretched lazily. "Was it worth the wait?"

He could hear the smile in her voice. "God, yes."

"I never realized it would be like this." She sounded tentative. "For weeks I've dreamed about it, but it always seemed like such a bad idea."

Weeks? He'd been thinking about it for years. Obsessing about it, yearning for it. After loving her from a distance all this time, he finally had her right where he wanted her. In his arms and in his bed. He wasn't about to let go. Shifting back a little, he lifted a few strands of long hair out of the way and kissed her neck.

"How does it seem now?"

She shivered. "It's looking a lot better."

"You don't sound a hundred percent sure about that."

"Convince me." Her voice was a husky invitation.

161

"Gladly." He rolled her onto her stomach and proceeded to trace a slow path down her back with his finger. He followed it with his tongue and when he reached the base of her spine, he kissed it.

She moaned. "Danny."

"Shh..."

He ran his fingers lightly over her buttocks, gently caressing her curves. She had a fine ass. He'd spent enough time studying it from behind, clothed. Being up close...well, he needed more time to get to know what it really looked liked. From where he was positioned, it looked good. Damn good. It was round and firm and gloriously feminine. He reached down and bit her left cheek.

"Ow." Her complaint was a low sigh, accompanied by a tiny shift. She spread her legs and lifted her hips, giving him an intimate view of her nether lips. She still gleamed from their combined juices.

Hunger engulfed him. So much for his soft dick.

He nuzzled her right butt cheek and she moaned. Her leg moved another inch, inviting further exploration. He wasn't one to refuse and dipped his hand between the toned cleft of her ass.

"Daniel..."

His first instinct was to bury his finger deep within her slick folds, but he didn't. He just looked, his mouth mere inches away. His cool breath steamed against her heat.

She groaned, her voice several tones lower than usual, and her buttocks clenched several times.

"Christ, Morgan. You're beautiful. So...hot. So...wet. I can hardly breathe when I look at you." He was almost dizzy from lack of air. Whatever oxygen he inhaled seemed to head straight to his cock.

"Daniel..."

He shushed her again as he reluctantly pulled away, saving the best for last. She squirmed beneath his hand as he made his way down her leg, pausing at the tender spot behind her knee to pay it special attention with butterfly-soft kisses. He continued his journey to her foot, massaging her toes until she shivered with pleasure.

When he was done with her feet, he rolled her over and began all over again.

"Do you have any idea how long I've wanted to taste you here?" He nibbled her neck before trailing kisses under her chin and followed an invisible line down to the bottom of her throat. "And here?" He nipped his way along her collarbone to her shoulder and back again.

He stopped when his head was poised above her breasts. For the longest time he simply stared, unable to move. Again, he was struck by the perfection of her breasts. They were firm and plump with dusky pink nipples that strained beneath his gaze. He tried to formulate a sentence but couldn't put the words together. Instead, a strangled noise escaped his throat as he dragged air into his lungs. If she only knew what he wanted to do to her breasts.

Before he could draw in another breath, she arched her back and thrust her chest upward. He rewarded her by cupping his hands around her plump flesh, leaving the nipples exposed. The vision of rosy buds peeping through his fingers was too good to resist, so he covered one puckered bud with his lips and rolled it around in his mouth, relishing the taste and the feel of it.

The sound of Amy's moan caught Daniel in his stomach. It tore through his gut and shot straight to his cock, leaving it

163

ramrod straight.

He took her other nipple in his mouth and subjected it to the same treatment. This time when she moaned, he bit her.

She yelped and wound her hands tightly through his hair.

"Did I hurt you?"

"Yes." His scalp stung when she pulled his hair, but it was nothing compared to the pain in his balls when she groaned, "Do it again."

Her nipples were even harder, and he nicked one with his teeth then immediately soothed it with his tongue. She writhed beneath his ministrations so he suckled hard on the other one, showing no mercy when she winced and cried, "Don't stop."

Stop? He was just getting started.

By the time Daniel lifted his head, he knew every inch of her breasts intimately. He knew what made her nipples bead and her breasts swell. He knew where to touch her to hear her groan and how to nip her so she screamed. And he also knew if he didn't stop then and there, he'd lose control completely. As it was, he teetered on the brink. If he licked her tits one more time or watched her writhe for another second, he'd climax without even fucking her.

Her hair was a tousled mess, her cheeks tinged pink. Green eyes were glazed with passion and her mouth puffed out tiny bursts of air. Christ, she was made for sex. Even her eyelashes turned him on. Long, thick and dark, they swept low over her eyes, enhancing the desire he saw there. Who could forget those lips? Those luscious, red lips, full and swollen from his kisses. They played havoc with his willpower. All he could think about was how they would feel wrapped around his cock. How they had felt, all warm, wet and hungry, when she went down on him. Five seconds. That's how long he'd last if she blew him now.

So he kissed her instead. He took her lips and proceeded to shake the foundations of his world with the intensity of his need. The velvety depths of her mouth left him mindless, the satiny heat of her tongue dazed him, and when at last he released her, she was a quivering mass beneath him. He was incapable of reason.

Instinct led him on.

He lowered his hand to her belly and with a feathery touch, skimmed it over her navel and the soft curve of her stomach until it rested on her mound. A light flick of his thumb over her clit and she was gasping, pushing hard against his hand. God, she was so responsive, so wet. His chest shuddered with wanting her. He kissed her again while he moved his thumb slowly, languidly, and dipped a finger into her moist heat.

Amy twisted and jerked beneath him.

Daniel released her mouth and cursed. If she so much as moaned, he'd lose it. In one fluid movement, he shifted down the mattress and replaced his thumb with his tongue.

She smelled of sex, musky and spicy. He fastened his mouth over her slit and kissed her, tasting himself on her lips. He just couldn't get enough. Tasting her—smelling her—was a heady aphrodisiac.

When she called his name, it came out as a long, low moan of pleasure. He thought he would burst a blood vessel trying to restrain himself.

He danced his tongue around her, swirling and tasting, until Amy thrashed on the bed, groaning unintelligibly. With a growing sense of satisfaction, he felt the tension build up in her. Several times she lifted her hips to meet his mouth. He increased the pressure and speed of his tongue, until she stiffened suddenly, threw her head back, and crumpled beneath him. Her orgasm was hard and long, and he kept his mouth fastened on her, lapping up her nectar as the spasms gradually lessened to light shudders and her breathing slowly returned to normal.

When at last she fell limp against the bed, he began his assault all over again. She bucked against his tongue and shook against his mouth. Her clit grew more engorged with every lick. She sobbed his name and within minutes he sensed her building up to another orgasm.

This time he wasn't so generous. He withdrew his tongue and pulled away from her only long enough to meld his mouth to hers. He lay along the length of her and with his knee, spread her legs further apart. The head of his cock touched the wet heat between her thighs and he almost came undone. Desire spiked through him, hot and fierce. He nudged his cock between her lips and she opened her thighs to welcome him in. Instead of plunging in like his need demanded he do, he held back.

Self-discipline was torturous.

With a will of iron, he pressed against her. Promising but not delivering, tormenting them both.

She whipped her head from side to side.

He pushed into her halfway then stopped and waited.

"Look at me," he whispered hoarsely. "I want to fuck you so bad, I'm losing control." He shook. He was out of his mind and he wanted her to see it, to understand the effect she had on him.

She opened her eyes and stared at him. Even in her lust-crazed state, he could see she understood his words. Her pupils were pinpricks of passion. "Do it," she urged. "Take me." With a neat shift of her butt, he found himself buried deep inside her.

Holy mother of—where in God's name did she learn that? He shuddered and grit his teeth. One more move like that and he'd

166

be history. He closed his eyes and counted to ten, then twenty. At twenty-three she repositioned herself and he slid in deeper. Her muscles clenched around him.

Christ, she is killing me.

There was nowhere on earth he'd rather be than where he was right now. When her muscles relaxed around him, he pulled out slowly and then glided back in. Moans filled his ears, but he wasn't sure whether they were his or hers. He really didn't care. Another thrust and he was moving in her, burying himself deep inside her welcoming warmth and then slowly pulling out again. Over and over as tension continued to build. Her eyes developed a glassy sheen. Sensation had taken over. She no longer saw him. Her breathing was shallow, punctuated by short, sharp gasps.

Damn, she was hot. Hot and sexy, his wet dream every night for months now. Only this time he was awake and she was real. He wasn't just dreaming about fucking her, he was fucking his dream girl.

Slow, restricted movements became impossible. He increased the tempo, driving into her as she raised her hips to meet his every thrust. Groaning out loud as her moans floated on wisps of air. She was wet, tight and so hot, he couldn't get enough. Harder and harder he moved, slamming into her.

When her muscles clamped down around him and she bucked, screaming her satisfaction, he stopped fighting the inevitable. He gave himself up to the force stampeding through him and exploded.

Chapter Eleven

"So that explains the little glint in your eye."

Amy repressed a smile and went to stand by her office window. "Just don't say I told you so."

"I told you so. God, I love it when I'm right."

She permitted Maggie her two-minute victory gloat. The woman had been right all along. The last ten days were proof of that.

"You should have listened to me from the start." Her face was gleeful as she launched into a lecture about how right she was. "It would've saved you both a lot of time. I can't believe it took you seventeen years to come to your senses."

Amy bit her lip and stared outside. "It's more a matter of taking a few months to lose my mind."

She heard Maggie sigh disbelievingly behind her. "You *still* think you made a mistake?"

She shrugged and turned to look at her friend. "I'm not sure. It's not as if I had much of a choice. There was so much chemistry between us, it was just a matter of time before one of us succumbed."

"Succumbed?" Maggie grinned. "Lady, from the sounds of it, you seduced the poor, innocent man. No two ways about it."

Bemused, she shook her head. Sure, she'd been the one to

strip, walk over and offer him her body, all unwrapped with the bow removed. But she didn't seduce him. Nope, if truth be known, *he* had been seducing *her* for months. Teasing and testing, titillating and tantalizing her until she'd finally come unglued—or, in this instance, undressed. By the time she wrung his little secret out of him, there was absolutely no doubt in her mind she would sleep with him.

"You know...I thought I had. The more I play it over in my head, the more I'm convinced he seduced me."

Maggie clapped her hands together. "He played you, didn't he?"

Amy smiled. "Like a fine-tuned instrument."

"Did he at least strike the right note?" The nurse winked.

As she relived their many hours of unbridled passion, she gave her friend a gratified grin. "Trust me. He had an entire symphony going there."

Maggie studied her with a knowing look. "Amy Morgan, I do believe you're in love."

Amy's world stood still.

What?

Her hands began to shake and her stomach lurched. She sat down and rested her head in her hands. *In love? With Daniel? Impossible.* Of course she loved him. Like a friend. But she wasn't *in* love with him.

Was she?

Oh...God. Holy crap. Shit. Shit, shit, shit! She was in love with him. Fully, whole-heartedly, completely and totally in love with him.

She would never have slept with him if she wasn't. It was one thing to risk their friendship by making love, it was completely another to flush it down the toilet. That's exactly

169

what she would have done if she been with him on a whim. No, sleeping with him had not been an impulsive move. It had been an ultimate expression of her feelings for him. From loving him in a purely platonic manner just a few short months ago, she now loved him in a very physical and intimate way.

The feeling disturbed her.

Astonished, she nodded. "Maggie McGill, I do believe you're right."

"Have you told him?"

"Christ, no."

"Why not?"

She didn't answer. What could she say? All she knew was that Daniel must never find out how she felt.

Maggie frowned. "This should be a happy time, a silly, goofy, stars-in-your-eyes time. Instead, you look as though you're being tortured. What's going on? Why the trepidation?"

Amy bit her lip. She *felt* tortured. Plagued with doubt. There were so many misgivings about her shifting relationship with Daniel, she could write a thesis on trepidation.

"Same old, same old, Mags. Daniel's not in this for the long haul. It's just a matter of time before he leaves me for someone else." Her anxiety at his inevitable departure ate away at her. They had become lovers. Everything was different. Soon Daniel would repeat his patterns of behavior. He'd grow bored with her, and he'd dump her. Like he dumped all his lovers. While part of her celebrated their newfound sexual relationship, another, more practical part wished it had never happened. "He's Mr. Run-From-Commitment. I'm scared if I told him how I felt, he'd bolt. He'd use the information as the perfect excuse to leave."

Maggie narrowed her eyes but didn't say anything.

Amy sighed dejectedly, squeezing her eyes shut against the inquisitive stare of her friend. "Besides, voicing my feelings out loud to him would make it too real, make me too vulnerable. If I expose my deepest emotion to him, it'll just hurt more when he does leave me."

"Amy, you already love him. Telling him isn't going to change that or make you love him any less. If he leaves you it's going to hurt, anyway you look at it. On the other hand, what if he loves you too? What if he plans to hang around? I think you're jumping the gun here, assuming he'll take off if he knows how you really feel."

Amy scowled. "He will leave, that's a given. It's just a matter of time." How many times had her mother told her father she loved him? Every day. He knew how dependent she was on him, how much she needed him. Did it help? No. Her father left anyway.

What about the asshole? She told him she loved him, even bared her soul to him. Simon still cheated on her.

As if reading her thoughts, Maggie said bluntly, "Cut the crap. He's *not* Simon. He would never hurt you."

Oh, Jeez. Maggie was right. Of course Daniel would never hurt her. Not deliberately anyway. No, he wasn't like her father or Simon. But he was Daniel. He had his routine. Love 'em and leave 'em. Only this time, it was her who was about to be left, and the thought made her sick to her stomach.

Amy swallowed down the wave of nausea. "A man doesn't have to be unfaithful to hurt you. Walking out on a lifetime together is just as bad. Worse."

"*If* he walks out. The guy's nuts about you. Anyone can see that. He'd rather die than hurt you."

"I know he'd never do it intentionally," she conceded. "But people don't just change overnight. Daniel doesn't do long-term

171

relationships. He won't change for me." He was a wonderful, wonderful man. But even wonderful men didn't modify their actions to suit their closest pal.

"For someone who claims to be his best friend, you don't have very much faith in him, do you?"

Once again, Maggie had floored her. As much as she loved Daniel, as much as she was in love with him, she simply didn't have faith in him. Not when it came to women. And as of now, she was officially one of *his* women.

She mulled over the idea. Was it possible he could change? Could he ever commit to being with her long-term? Did she even want a long-term commitment from him?

She'd never given it much deliberation. Never thought that far in advance. She always assumed he'd be in her life as her friend. On the other hand, she always assumed that if they ever slept together, he'd dump her and their friendship. She never considered the possibility that they might be a—oh Lord, could she say it?—a couple. A real couple in a real relationship.

She shook her head, intuitively knowing it could never happen. Even if Daniel did change, even if he did make a commitment to her, she'd never fully trust him, never fully believe he wanted to be with her and only her. She would spend her days living in doubt about his staying power. Experience had taught her men did not stay with her. It didn't matter what Daniel intended to do or how he intended to behave because, Amy realized, *she* was the one who couldn't change. She could never accept a relationship based on mistrust. And that's what she'd do. Mistrust him. Every day of their lives.

A relationship between the two of them would never work. There were too many variables working against them. There was Daniel's inability to commit, and her inability to trust him. In that moment Amy came to a conclusion. It was the only conclusion she could arrive at based on her insight into their personalities. She had to end their affair soon. Taking their relationship any further than it had already gone would destroy them completely. It would ruin any chance they had of resuming their friendship.

It wasn't fair, she thought with a heavy heart. She wasn't ready to let go of him just yet. She had only just discovered the wonderful world of sex with Daniel, and wonderful sex it was. Wonderful, marvelous, mind-blowing, orgasmic sex. With Daniel, the most mundane actions became super-incredible sexual experiences.

With Daniel, she turned into a fiery sex kitten, a woman with a voracious appetite for making love. Daniel's hunger, it would seem, was just as insatiable as hers. No opportunity was frowned upon or overlooked. When they could make love, they did. And they did it frequently.

Take last night for instance. A mundane, everyday occurrence had turned into red-hot passion frenzy. They were sitting companionably in his lounge, she doing a crossword, he reading, when she'd accidentally dropped her pen and had to crouch down on the floor to pull it out from under her chair.

"Don't move an inch," Daniel rasped.

On her hands and knees, her butt stuck in the air, she looked over her shoulder at him and was blinded by the raw desire playing across his face.

"Not an inch." He unbuttoned his jeans and walked towards her.

She watched, powerless to move, her breath coming in short, sharp gasps as he shucked his pants and knelt behind her.

Right there on the floor, he lifted her skirt, shoved her thong aside and fucked her from behind. She took every last pulsing inch of him, crying out his name until she finally collapsed under him, her body and his a writhing mass of post-orgasmic bliss.

It was things like that she wasn't ready to give up yet. Things like that she needed a little more time to enjoy.

Amy looked at Maggie. "You're right. I don't have much faith in him, or myself. I just don't see us going anywhere." She shook her head. "But that's okay. For now, I'm going to make the most of what little time we do have." She intended to spend all their remaining time together discovering new things about her old friend. Take the time to enjoy Daniel, enjoy loving him and enjoy making love with him. Just enough to give her a whole arsenal of good memories so when the day came Daniel did move on, or when she decided she couldn't live with the doubt any longer, she would at least have her memories to keep her warm at night.

$$\wp$$

"Hi." He lounged in her doorway, eyeing her hungrily. A huge grin was plastered across his face.

"Hi yourself." She stared at him, unable to get enough.

"You ready to leave?"

"In a minute." Her voice was a breathy invitation.

"In a minute," he agreed. In one lithe movement, he swept down and devoured her mouth.

"Mmm..." Her heart thudded. She wound her arms around his neck, arching into him.

He kicked the door shut and his arm crept around her waist, drawing her close. She sighed into his mouth as his tongue plundered hers. Her whole body reverberated in pleasure.

"Sorry I'm late." Daniel trailed warm, moist kisses down her neck.

"S'okay." She threw her head back to allow him easier access to the sensitive spot beneath her ear.

"If we leave now we can just make the nine o'clock show." He nibbled the edge of her earlobe.

"What should we see?" She moaned softly as her hands snuck under his shirt and kneaded the velvety flesh of his stomach, relishing the hard muscle below.

"The new Tom Hanks movie started yesterday." His fingers made short work of her buttons, undoing her top and pushing it open. He inhaled deeply as he gazed at her breasts, his lower lip caught between his teeth.

Her nipples strained against her bra, pebbling into tight buds. She shuddered as his mouth closed over one. "I hear he's...very good in it. Oh!" The sensation of his hot, wet tongue over the lacy lingerie sent her body temperature soaring.

"The reviews have been okay." He turned his attention to the other breast, laving the flesh buried beneath the lace.

She gasped. "Where's it showing?" The zip on his jeans caught as she tugged on it with shaking hands. Forcing herself to slow down, she eased the zip over his straining erection and pushed the flaps aside. She covered him with her hand.

"At the, ah...cinemas." He pulsated under her fingers.

"I know." She nipped his shoulder then licked away the sting, enjoying the taste of his salty skin. "Which one?"

Her shirt lay beside his on the floor and her bra followed seconds later. She dipped her hand beneath the elastic of his boxer shorts and wrapped her fingers around him.

He jerked into her. "Uh...the one where they...oh

175

man...show films." His voice was rough and his breathing ragged.

"We should probably go soon." She knelt before him and pushed his pants down his legs.

"Yeah. We don't want to..." He cursed, his voice thick. "We...don't want to..."

The soft wool of the carpet cushioned her knees and the cool air teased her bare breasts. "We don't want to what?" She licked her way up his shaft.

Smoky, hooded eyes absorbed her actions. "We don't want to miss the, um...whaddaya call it." A muscle worked in his jaw.

"The beginning?" She took the head of his cock in her mouth and swirled her tongue around it.

"Yes..." He sank his hands into her hair. "We don't want to miss the beginning."

"No," she agreed. "We...wouldn't...want to...do that." She opened her mouth wide and sucked in his full length.

They missed the whole film.

℘

Amy lay curled on her side on the carpet next to Daniel, his arms wrapped around her, holding her close. Idly, she circled her fingertips over his chest. "It's weird, isn't it?"

"What?" His eyes were closed as he questioned her.

"Us. This."

"S'not weird. S'nice." His voice was rich and low. "In fact." Eyes now open, he turned his head to kiss her. "It's perfect."

She couldn't have agreed more. "Yeah, but still...you'd think it would be weird between us. You'd think we'd feel, I don't know, inhibited maybe?"

"You weren't inhibited a few moments ago." A smile stirred his sleepy features.

Amy poked him. "Well, that's just my point. I take one look at you and all I want to do is tear your clothes off and make wild love with you. I can't seem to keep you at arm's length anymore." She paused and puckered her brow. "I don't know how I ever did."

"Ah, babe, I don't know why you ever wanted to." He kissed her again, a long, slow, lazy kiss. It was so intoxicating she forgot what she'd been saying. His lips drugged her, sent her drifting off to nowhere. When he pulled away, she came floating back to earth.

"You never asked why I was late tonight."

"I didn't think about it." She stretched sluggishly and yawned, then burrowed into his warmth. "I assumed you got sidetracked taking photos."

"Uh-uh. I was busy. With two things."

"Two?"

"Yep. First off, I went to the hospital, to see Vicky."

"And?" Since their trip to POWS a few weeks back she hadn't been able to get her mind off the child.

"And she's being discharged tomorrow."

Amy's smile matched the one she could hear in his voice. "That is wonderful news."

"I know. I'm totally psyched about it. So is her mother. Things are looking up for the family."

She knew Daniel's relief was enormous. "I'm happy for her. And for you." She squeezed his arm. "What was the other thing that happened today?"

"I had a surprise visitor."

"Anyone I know?" She would have lifted her head to show her interest, but she was just too drowsy, content and happy lying where she was.

"Janine Stillman."

Amy's senses sharpened. "From National Geographic?"

"Uh-huh." His voice vibrated with restrained excitement.

She sat up, suddenly paying close attention. "She's in Sydney?" Janine lived in San Francisco. What was she doing here?

"Yup. On a two week holiday before she starts a new assignment."

"For the magazine?" Janine had worked with Daniel on a spread for National Geographic a couple of years back. The two had done a brilliant piece on Sydney, with Janine authoring the article and Daniel providing the pictures.

Daniel nodded. "And guess what?"

"What?" She stared at him, apprehension prickling the base of her spine. When Daniel and Janine had completed the article and sent it in for publication, they'd honored their accomplishment with a little celebratory sex. Four solid days of celebratory sex. Daniel hadn't even taken time out to answer his phone.

"National Geographic has offered me a second assignment. They want me to do the photographs." A grin split his face and his eyes danced.

Amy felt sick and thrilled at the same time. She fought to keep her voice animated as the contents of her belly swirled uneasily. "Fantastic! Tell me more."

"It's an article looking at the beaches of New South Wales, from the Sapphire Coast all the way up to Byron Bay. We'll choose about ten of the best. Visit them, film them, interview the locals, get to know the places a bit better and then come back and put the whole piece together."

"Sounds amazing." It did. He loved working for the magazine. He would never refuse an opportunity to do a shoot for them again.

She wanted to throw up.

Daniel jumped up. "I know. I feel like a kid I'm so excited."

"Where will you stay?" Although she really did not want to hear the answer, it was politic to keep up the charade.

"The magazine's organized hotels or bed and breakfasts at various towns. We just need to phone with the dates."

How many rooms will they need? "When do you start?" Anxiety threatened to overwhelm her.

"If I take the job, two weeks Monday, after Janine's holiday. I'd be away for about a month. I know it's a long time, but we think it would be better if we did all the traveling in one go rather than break it into smaller trips."

Two weeks. She had two weeks left with Daniel and then he'd leave with Janine. He'd be leaving, period. Two weeks until Daniel left her heart and their friendship shattered into a million pieces.

A fist squeezed around her heart, tighter and tighter, causing such pain it left Amy breathless.

"What do you mean *if* you take the job? Of course you have to take it. It's an opportunity of a lifetime. You know you want it more than anything else."

He sat back down again and looked at her, his expression serious. "Morgan, this isn't just anyone I'll be working with. It's Janine. None of us—not you, not me and not Janine—is stupid enough to ignore our history. I've slept with her."

The invisible fist held her heart in a death grip.

She had known all along this thing with Daniel would end, she just hadn't expected it to happen so quickly. What could she do? She couldn't pretend Daniel hadn't just laid his cards on the table. She couldn't ignore what he just said.

She stared blankly at him, feeling the blood drain from her face.

He grabbed her hand. "I won't do this without your consent, Morgan. I won't go unless it's one hundred percent okay with you."

Fucking hell. What did he want? Her permission to sleep with Janine again? If Daniel went on this assignment, there was no way in hell it would remain platonic. Not with their past. Not with their present—a month away, exploring gorgeous coastlines, staying in romantic hotels, in who knew how many rooms...

"Danny, you have to go. This is National Geographic you're talking about. It's not some arbitrary project that wouldn't matter to you one way or another. Of course you must do it." Every fiber of her being fought her words, ralling together to suppress them. She hated giving him her approval.

As much as she loathed admitting it, it was the right thing to do. Daniel would never forgive himself if he passed up the assignment. She'd never forgive herself for forcing him to.

His eyes searched her face. "You sure?"

"Of course I am. You have to do it."

"Amy, Janine and I were lovers."

Shut up. Shut up, shut up! "Danny, it's National Geographic."

He didn't answer her straight away. He just looked at her as if trying to read any underlying meaning behind her expression.

She forced a huge smile into place. "National Geographic," she reiterated. "How can you even think of turning them down?"

"But Janine..."

"Do the article."

"You sure?" Doubt clouded his eyes.

"Say yes."

"Morgan..." His expression was still doubtful although his eyes gleamed hopeful.

"Do it!"

He nodded. "I'll do it."

"Good." *No...bad. Very, very bad.* She wrapped her arms around him and hugged him close. Partly to show him her happiness for him, but mainly to hide her utter desolation.

Amy was no fool. She knew exactly what she'd just done. She gave Daniel her permission to sleep with Janine. Signed, sealed and delivered.

Chapter Twelve

She was living in hell. From the moment Daniel had mentioned that woman's name, life had been a bitch. Amy was on the mother of all rollercoaster rides—emotionally speaking. From the extreme euphoria of loving Daniel to the profound sense of impending doom, she experienced the entire spectrum of emotions.

The pleasure she usually felt around him was tainted by rage and jealousy churning in her stomach. Sure, she was happy when she was with him. How could she not be? Just looking at him made her smile, and lifted her spirits. Stirred her body to life. Then she'd think about Janine and bam, she was miserable all over again.

She'd only met the woman once or twice, but darn, she hated her. Hated everything about her. And especially hated what she represented. The end of her and Daniel's relationship.

All she had left with Daniel was one weekend and then he was going away with *her*. His ex-lover. His *future* lover.

She gave up fighting, gave up arguing with herself. While half of her wanted to beg Daniel to stay, to give up his dreams and work and stay in Sydney with her, the other half, the more pragmatic half, knew it was over. It was that half that had just won the final argument.

Spending another weekend with Daniel was futile. Why

prolong the agony? Her mind was made up. She had to end their fling.

When he arrived at her place, she'd tell him. It would shred her heart into thousands of pieces, but at least she'd be taking a stand. Dumping him before he dumped her. Giving him the freedom to fuck Janine Stillman, or whatever other women he wanted to fuck. Just not her anymore.

Who knew? After all was said and done, maybe they could even go back to being friends again. They'd done it before, after the exhibition. Maybe they could do it again.

She'd like that. It probably wasn't possible, but she'd like that.

The doorbell rang.

Her hands shook as she rubbed them over her tired eyes. Taking a deep, fortifying breath to brace her for what was about to happen, she opened the door and let Daniel in. *Lord!* Why did he have to look so sexy? Why did he have to stand there in the doorway, undressing her with those smoky eyes?

"Ah, babe. Just seeing you makes me hard."

Damn it, couldn't he say hello like a normal person? Did *she* have to get so turned on just looking at him?

He leaned in close and pressed his lips to hers. "Do we have to make small talk or can we just strip and make love right here on the floor?" He wound his hand through her hair and slipped his tongue into her mouth.

Pain sliced through her belly as she reacted instinctively, kissing him back. She responded on the most primal level. Her body grew slick with need and her breasts swelled. For a very long time all they did was kiss, she prolonging what was, in all likelihood, their last one.

He pulled away and pressed a single red rose into her

hand.

Her fingers wound round the stem, clutching it. God, she wanted to make love to him. But she couldn't. If she did, she'd never find the strength to do what she was about to.

She held the rose to her nose and breathed in deeply. "Daniel..." What could she say?

"This rose is just the first of many. I intend to have a rose a day delivered to your home while I'm away. Just to make sure you don't forget me while I'm gone."

Fat chance. Amy suspected that every minute of every day he was away, she'd be obsessing about what he was doing. Whom he was doing it with.

She shook her head, almost choking over her words. "Dan, we need to talk."

His smile vanished. "About what?"

"Let's sit down." She chose a single high-backed seat, not trusting herself to share a couch with him. "Um...thank you for the flower." Maybe if they started on neutral ground she could find the courage to move on from there.

Instead of sitting on the couch, he knelt in front of her. He took her empty hand, held it in his and looked into her eyes. "It's a rose, Morgan, not just a flower. A red rose. A symbol of love."

Her breath caught and struggled to escape. Her lungs felt like they were ready to explode if she didn't exhale. She couldn't move. All she could do was wait, suspended in what felt like another dimension, a parallel universe.

"Because I love you." His eyes shone. Love seemed to pour out of them. She saw it all there—all her hopes and dreams—reflected in his eyes. For a minute she allowed it to wash over her. Allowed herself the wonder of being loved by Daniel. It felt like the only thing she ever wanted. It made everything right. She loved him too. For that minute, her world was whole.

Then she exhaled. Her lungs jolted and she breathed again. As the breath left her body, that impossible parallel universe fizzled away. Fresh oxygen hit her brain and brought with it the cold reality of the moment. Daniel might think he loved her, and much as she wished, *wished* it were true, she knew better.

Her sigh slammed into Daniel's gut and he braced himself. Instinctively he knew whatever Amy was about to say he did not want to hear.

"Danny." Her eyes were closed. "You're confusing physical attraction for love. You don't love me. We're good friends who sleep together. That's not love, that's sex."

What the fuck? He wasn't the slightest bit confused about his feelings for her. He loved her. Always had. Always would. What part of "I love you" didn't she understand?

"Amy," he began, when he trusted himself to talk evenly. "When you and I sleep together, we are not having sex. We're making love."

She shook her head. "No. It just feels that way. It's easy to mistake passion for love. Especially since we know each other so well. We love each other like friends and desire each other like lovers. It doesn't mean you love me."

He stared at her. *Was she crazy? What the fuck did she think it meant?* "I love you and I desire you. What more is there?"

She sighed again. "Nothing. Everything."

"Care to be a little more specific?" He knew what was coming.

"We have to end this...this thing between us. Now, before

it's too late."

"Too late for what?" *Where was the air in this room?*

"For us. For me. For you."

"Lady, I don't have a clue what you're talking about." But he did. And it was killing him. Everything he worked so hard for, everything he achieved was about to come crashing down. She didn't love him. Not like he loved her, anyway.

He hadn't just dared to hope her feelings for him had changed, he'd come to believe it with all of his heart. Amy had given herself to him totally. Once they had finally crossed the line and slept together, she'd surrendered her body to him with the ease of a lover and the trust of a best friend. When he and Amy made love they were closer than they'd ever been. They were like one person.

He had truly believed she'd fallen in love with him, truly believed they had made the transition from mates to soul mates.

He was wrong. His plan had failed. All he'd managed to do was get her into bed—and now she was climbing out, alone.

Her voice, when she spoke, was bland. "If we end it now, there's still a chance we can go back to being friends. If we don't, one of us is going to get hurt. If that happens, I don't think we can save our friendship."

Too late. He was already hurting. Hell, having a knife stuck in his back and twisting it would be less painful.

Didn't she understand he would never hurt her? How could he? He loved her. Hadn't he been clear enough in his feelings for her? "You don't get it, do you? You never have. You think all of this between us is just physical."

She shrugged. "I do get it. I'm seriously attracted to you and you wanted to sleep with me. The decision to do it was mutual. It was good while it lasted, but it's over now."

"You think that's what all this is about? A little uncomplicated sex? A quick fuck and then back to being friends?"

"You made your needs very clear. From the night of the exhibition to the day at your pool, you were quite clear about what you wanted from me."

Not clear enough, obviously. "You're kidding right?" This had to be some kind of a bad joke.

Amy shook her head.

He stared at her, his jaw hanging open in disbelief. How had she got things so wrong? "Think about it, Morgan. Our relationship changed after you met Vicky. Remember that? You wanted to know what I'd discussed with her and my answer was you."

A pained look crossed Amy's face as she nodded.

"What exactly do you think I said to her? D'ya think I told a ten-year-old child, with leukemia, no less, that I wanted to fuck my friend and what did she think about the idea?"

She spluttered. "I...oh! God, no."

He was on a roll now, spurred on by a burning anger. "Picture it, me sitting with Vicky and telling her every time I saw you I got so turned on all I could think about was screwing you. Does that sound like me? *Does it?*"

Amy stared at him, aghast, and he knew he took the unpleasant image too far. He silently counted to ten, forced himself to calm down. "Damn it, Morgan. I told her she inspired me to change my life, to change my ways. I told her that her strength and her will to live and enjoy life made me want to live my life to the fullest, and that I could only do that with you." He stopped and looked at her, filled with despair. "A ten-year-old can understand my feelings for you, why can't you?"

She stared at him, her eyes bright with tears. Still he could see the resolve on her face. She was slipping through his fingers and there was nothing he could do about it.

"Amy, I don't want to be your friend. We've been friends for seventeen years. It's not enough anymore. I want more. I want it all. I want to be your lover, your confidant and your partner. I want you. All of you."

"Oh Danny, don't say things like that. You can't expect me to believe you when you talk this way." A tear slid down her cheek. "I know how emotional you were with Vicky, I know how involved you got with her and I'm sure she inspired you. But I don't think you're being realistic. I don't think you love me. I think you like the idea of it though. I know you, you'll grow bored. You're not capable of the kind of commitment real love entails. I can't take the risk of becoming more involved with you."

"Risk? You think I'm a risk?" He nodded as realization dawned on him. Her past was coming back to haunt them. "You think I'm like Simon. You think I'll hurt you, just like he did. Betray you, cheat on you."

She shrugged. "I think you'll leave. You always do."

He narrowed his eyes, reluctant to bring her father into the argument but knowing he had no choice. "I'm not your father, either. You're not your mother. Our relationship is different." He calmed himself, kept his tone gentle. "Morgan, I understand you've been hurt before, felt rejected by the men you love. But I'm different. You *know* that. Hello? It's me, Danny, your friend. Remember, the one you've counted on your whole life? The one who's been there for you, when *those* men weren't? Damn it, you turned to me for support when Simon cheated, you came to me for sympathy when your dad left. I was there for you. I'll *always* be there for you."

Amy was crying openly now, tears pouring down her cheeks. "As my friend," she sobbed. "You were there as my friend. I could trust you then. I knew you wouldn't betray me. I could lean on you." She sniffed loudly and wiped her nose on her arm. "But it's different now," she whispered.

"Why?" He was stumped. "Because we're sleeping together? You trust me less because I'm not just your friend but your lover as well?"

She nodded. "You leave your lovers, Dan. You always do. I don't want to be one of those women you leave."

"I'm not leaving you, Morgan."

"Yes, you are. On Monday."

Understanding broke through. "Son of a bitch," he swore, his anger escalating. "It's all about Janine, isn't it? You think I'm gonna sleep with her." He was pissed off. "What the heck? I've slept with her before, I'll sleep with her again. A little mindless fucking to while away the long nights together." He was damn furious. "What the hell kind of trust do you have in me, anyway?" He jumped up and paced the room, his voice way louder than usual. "We discussed this." He jabbed a finger in her direction. "I asked you if you were okay with me and Janine working together. Several times. What was your response? 'Do it, Danny. You have to do it.'" He whipped his hand through his hair. "You told me to go ahead. No, you insisted!"

The deep breath he took didn't relax him in the slightest. He stalked over to Amy and leaned over her, his hands gripping the arms of the chair. "Just what the fuck kind of an opinion do you have of me, anyway? Do you seriously think I'd sleep with another woman just because I can? Because the opportunity is there?"

Amy opened her mouth then closed it without saying

189

anything.

"Do I mean so little to you?" His voice was hoarse. He couldn't help it. Her lack of trust was nothing less than astounding. "We've been together for seventeen years and you think I'd screw around on you? Dump you to screw someone else? You think I'd fuck you over like that?" She honestly thought he would. How could she have so damn little faith in him, in them? "You're an idiot—and a hypocrite. You're the one who's running here. Not me. You're the one who's scared of commitment. You're breaking up with me before I can break up with you."

He shook his head in contempt. "We could have it all. We could have our friendship, we could be lovers... Hell, somewhere down the line we could even have a family. But you're so scared I may hurt you, you're not even willing to give us a chance."

Amy seemed to spring back to life. "If I gave you a chance it would destroy me. Maybe I am scared. So what? My fears are justified. Your past proves you can't commit to a woman. When was the last time you had a meaningful relationship? Why should I believe ours would be different?" Her voice lifted a notch. "You'll leave me, Daniel, just like my father and just like Simon. When you do, I'll lose it all. My lover and my best friend. I can't do it. I'm not strong enough to cope with it. You will leave, Daniel, you always do."

Daniel pushed himself away from her chair. "Damn it, Amy. Have a bit of faith."

She shook her head sadly. "I can't take the chance."

He grabbed both of her wrists, desperate. "Trust me."

"Danny, in the last two years alone you've had fourteen—no, fifteen girlfriends. I refuse to be one of those women. I couldn't bear the rejection when it was time to move on."

He shook her arms. "Open your eyes, woman. We have a history together, a friendship that will secure this relationship. I love you. Why would I ever leave you?"

Amy put up her hand. "Stop it. Don't say things like that. It just makes it more difficult for me to end this."

"Why would you want to end it?" Was he the only one who could see how illogical this was?

"Because I don't want to be hurt again," she snapped. "And I will be if this goes any further."

"You haven't heard a word I've said. I won't hurt you. I love you." He was shouting now.

"No. You love the idea of me. You love me as a friend and you love making love to me. That doesn't mean you're in love with me."

"What more do you want me to do?" he yelled. "What else can I say to convince you I'm dead serious?" He pounded the wall in frustration. "For God's sake, Amy, we're adults. Don't you think I know what I mean when I say I love you? Don't you think it's time you put a little faith in me?"

He watched her face ice over, watched as her shoulders stiffened and her back straightened. Before his eyes she turned into a stranger.

She uttered the words that made him sick to his stomach. "I think, Daniel, that it's time to call it quits. If we continue to sleep together, I'll only end up resenting you and I'd hate that. Please leave. Now. While our friendship is still intact. So our memories of this...time aren't twisted and bitter, so that tomorrow when we wake up, we can be friends again."

"Don't do this, Amy. Don't destroy us. We don't deserve that." Anguish tore at his gut.

"It's too late, Daniel. It's over. Please, just leave."

Pain. So much pain. How was it possible to feel so fucked up from one conversation?

"Please," she begged him. "Please go. While I still have some dignity left."

"We won't be friends tomorrow." He could never go back. "I don't want to be your friend. It's not enough, not anymore." Did he sound as god-awful as he felt?

She never answered, just crossed the room and opened the door.

What more was there to say? Daniel walked to the door, stopped, turned around and took one last look at her. Then he left. The soft click of the door closing behind him echoed throughout his hollow body.

Chapter Thirteen

When Simon cheated on her, Amy thought she'd never get over it. Thought she would be miserable and alone for the rest of her life. Time had taught her the truth. The heartache she dealt with after Simon left was nothing compared to what she was going through now. It was like comparing a blister to an amputation.

What she was experiencing now was nothing short of absolute destruction. Daniel had been ripped out of her life. One minute he was there and everything was fantastic. The next he was gone and her whole world was just one big screwup.

Without Daniel, she had nothing. Life lost all meaning.

When he walked out of her apartment, he walked out of her life. There were no negotiations, no "I'll see you tomorrow", no last minute change of mind. He was gone. Her brilliant plan had failed. She hadn't saved herself from the hurt of his ultimate rejection, and she hadn't saved any part of their friendship.

Without meaning to, she fulfilled her own prophecy. She lost her lover and her best friend. All because she sent him away.

Bottom line: she messed up. Messed up bad.

She couldn't sleep properly, couldn't even remember the last time she had a full night's rest. She would lie in bed and ache for the feel of Daniel's warm body against hers, the sound of his voice in her ear as they made love.

When she did sleep, her dreams were troubled. They were always about Daniel, but she could never talk to him in them, never touch him. He was always too far away or had just left when she arrived. She would yell, try to catch his attention, but her screams would find no voice. When she tried to run after him, her legs were weighted and wouldn't move. He would always walk away, walk out of her life, and she was helpless to get him back.

It was easier not to sleep.

Food lost its appeal. It stuck in her throat, gagging her. In the passing weeks she lost nearly nine pounds.

It was easier not to eat.

Then there were those terrifying moments when she couldn't remember what he looked like. She could feel his silky curls, smell his aftershave, even see his dimples and devilish smile, but she couldn't put the image together to make his face whole.

It had been a month now, the most awful month of her life. A month of silence. She didn't have a clue whether his assignment was over or even if he was home. She hadn't heard a word from him since that hideous night. Not a visit, not a call, not even an SMS.

She couldn't blame him. After all, she kicked him out. What did she want him to do? Come groveling back to her? Daniel didn't grovel.

There wasn't a damn thing she could do to get him back.

Amy missed him. Hell, she pined for him. She was lonelier than she ever thought possible. Even when she stood in the middle of a crowd, she was alone. Her best friend was gone. She had sent her lover away and life was just plain crap.

How could she have coordinated this terrible sequence of events? How could she have calmly stood in her lounge and ordered Daniel out of her life? Her reasoning had seemed so solid then. Now it just seemed stupid. Shit, her whole life was stupid, pointless.

Without Daniel, it held no purpose.

She loved the man. Wanted him back. She couldn't live without him. Her sorry state of mind bore testament to that fact.

A knock on the door disturbed her despondent musings.

"Come in!" She blotted her eyes and blew her nose, clearing her throat as she stared expectantly at the door.

Maggie walked in with Miranda, one of the other fertility counselors.

"Hi Ame, we need your help, if that's—" Maggie broke off mid-sentence and stared at Amy.

Amy shook her head, hoping Maggie would understand she didn't want to say anything right now, especially in front of Miranda. "Hayfever," she lied.

Maggie looked uncertain for a moment, even opened her mouth a few times to say something, but in the end she gave a short nod and simply said, "We were hoping to get your help with this case, if you have the time."

"Of course." She temporarily shoved her misery aside, figuring she had about four minutes until the pain came reeling through again. "Come sit down."

Maggie handed her a folder. "I know you're familiar with the basic details of the case," she said. "But there's been a new development."

Without even glancing at the folder, Amy knew they were talking about the gay couple.

"Maggie and I have just had a meeting with them," Miranda said. "They've decided to go ahead with artificial insemination through the clinic. They're using a known donor, a gay friend of theirs."

"Are they fully aware of the legal rights the man will have once the child is born?" Amy asked.

"Fully. So is the donor. That's why we're here. We all think he should have counseling before he donates his sperm. Although he has indicated his willingness to give up his parental rights, both women want to make sure he is one hundred percent okay with his choice."

"And you want me to counsel him?"

Miranda nodded. "It wouldn't be ethical for me to counsel him, not when I've seen the couple. He needs someone objective."

Amy nodded. "I'll do it with pleasure." She had wished she was involved in this case and now here was her opportunity. Besides, it would give her something to focus on, apart from Daniel. "What timeframe are we looking at?"

"The sooner you see him, the sooner we can start the treatment," Maggie said.

"All the details are in here?" She held up the file.

Miranda nodded.

"Okay, I'll read through it now and give him a call. Is he expecting to hear from me?"

"He knows someone's going to contact him," Miranda said, standing up.

"I'll let you know what happens," she promised as Miranda left. Maggie didn't move.

With Miranda no longer in the office, Amy's defenses dropped.

"Still feel shitty?"

"Worse," Amy admitted. "And don't be nice, it'll only make me cry." It was too late though. Her tears were already starting.

"Call him," Maggie urged. "Tell him you made a mistake. Ask him for a second chance."

She shook her head. "I can't. He doesn't want to hear from me. If he did, he'd have contacted me."

"Bull," Maggie contradicted her. "You kicked him out...right after he told you he loved you. Why would he try get in touch?"

"He doesn't love me." She felt her heart heave again and she blotted her eyes. "If he did, he would have phoned, he would have tried. The truth is he's relieved. He's free to sleep with other women. With...with that journalist. I bet he's having the time of his life." The last sentence resonated with bitterness.

Maggie frowned at her. "You really dealt Daniel a bad hand, didn't you? You've been bloody unfair to him. I know you're hurting, but how do you think he feels? His closest friend suddenly decides she doesn't want to see him again. The woman he loves kicks him out. He laid his heart on the line and what do you say? He's talking crap? Exactly how much rejection do you think one guy can take?"

"How much rejection can I take?" She refused to acknowledge Maggie's point. "I've already been dumped by one man I loved." Even as she said it she knew she didn't give a damn about Simon or his actions any longer. Her only concern was Daniel. "I can't risk it happening again, especially with someone who means so much to me."

"So without giving him a chance, you dump him."

"You're not being very sympathetic."

"You're not being very logical," Maggie rebutted. "For weeks now I've comforted you and been on your side, but there's another side to all of this. There's Daniel's side. I suspect he's just as miserable as you are. If you weren't so stubborn, you'd see that."

"Daniel's glad to have his freedom. He's busy with Janine." Images of what Daniel might be doing with Janine floated across her vision, sending sparks of pain into her heart.

"Daniel is not Simon."

"He's still a man."

"A man you're in love with."

"He'll hurt me." She refused to see Maggie's point of view.

"You're already hurting and Daniel had nothing to do with it."

"He has everything to do with it."

"Just do me a favor," Maggie said as she stood up. "Think about what I've said. You're miserable, plain and simple. The only way you'll feel happy again is if you and Daniel get back together. Phone him."

"That's it?" Amy stared at Maggie as she opened the office door. "You're giving me orders and walking out?"

Maggie shrugged. "I have a patient and you're being stubborn. You love him, phone him." She closed the door behind her.

"Yeah and risk having him tell me he's sleeping with Janine Stillman now." She'd rather stick toothpicks in her eyes.

The file Miranda left behind lay on her desk. She may be feeling terrible but duty still called. She opened the file and a notebook and proceeded to make detailed notes of the case as she read.

The patient, Annie Brauer, a journalist with one of the local newspapers, had made contact with the clinic, requesting details about artificial insemination using donor sperm. Maggie saw her and her partner for the first time about three months ago and made thorough notes about their meeting.

Annie and her partner...

Amy gaped at the sheet in her hand, sure she misread vital information. She shook her head, snapped her jaw closed and reread Annie's partner's name. Then she went over each detail of the case with meticulous care, reading the file from cover to cover. When she finished, she leaned back in her chair and spluttered in disbelief. For the first time in a month, she began to laugh.

Miranda would have to pass the case on to Olivia. Amy couldn't do the counseling.

It was unethical to get involved in cases where she knew the patients personally. Annie Brauer's long-term partner was a pediatric oncologist at Sydney's Eastern Suburbs Hospital. Her name was Leona Ramsey.

∞

Well, well, well. Amy left work, bewildered at the unexpected turn of events. Some days were more interesting than others. Some days, you learned a whole lot of information that you never expected.

Daniel's married admirer was a lesbian and thus, by logical conclusion, not interested in men. Not even hot, sexy and devilishly handsome men like Daniel.

He concocted a whole convoluted plan to throw Leona off his back, when—let's face facts here—she was never on his back in the first place. Come on. No woman planning to start a family with her female lover would try to seduce a man. It just didn't work like that. Sure, it was almost every man's fantasy to seduce or be seduced by a lesbian—and hopefully her girlfriend as well—but that's all it was. A fantasy.

Duh!

So what the hell was Daniel thinking? Why did he insist she kiss him when there was really no reason? Daniel must have known Leona was gay. According to the notes in the file, their relationship wasn't secret. Their friends and colleagues were well aware of the situation. Leona and Lexi were friends *and* colleagues, so Lexi would know about Annie. If Lexi knew then surely she would have told Daniel.

If Daniel knew Leona was a lesbian, why did he tell Amy she was married? Maybe she and Annie *were* married, but from the way Daniel had put it, she believed Leona was married to a man.

She kissed Daniel to help him blow off Leona. He concocted a whole scheme to get rid of her, using Amy as the decoy. But Leona was a lesbian. It didn't make sense.

Everything had changed the night Daniel kissed her. That first kiss set off a whole tidal wave of reaction. And need. And lust. And sex. All it took was one kiss and she was hooked. She no longer just wanted to be friends. She wanted to be her best friend's lover and she wanted it bad.

There was no doubt about it, the feelings had been reciprocated.

Amy paused midstep. What if Daniel *did* know Leona was gay? What if he made the whole story up? What if Leona was in on the conspiracy?

"Well, I'll be..." She spoke out loud as comprehension dawned on her. "He set the whole thing up."

She'd been duped by her own best friend. Leona wasn't interested in him. It had nothing to do with the woman. Daniel was interested in her. Amy. Had been all along. He plotted and schemed to get her interested in him and he neatly organized it so she would have no choice but to kiss him.

That night on the beach he put her in a rather tricky situation, explaining the details of Leona's lust for him and then begging her to help him. Leona must have been privy to his plans all along. Who knows, she may have even enjoyed playing the seductive doctor. Amy fell for it. She instinctively felt the need to come to Daniel's rescue so when he kissed her, she kissed him right back. He must have known she would never kiss him under any other circumstances, so he planned the whole damned thing.

Her head spun. Why didn't he just come right out and tell her how he felt? Why didn't he just kiss her?

Because she wouldn't have taken him seriously, that's why. She would have stopped him before he ever got the chance to start. She would have been too amused or too perplexed, even too damn afraid to ever let him finish. She would have fiercely protected their friendship, refusing to allow any other factors to interfere.

This way he insinuated their romance into her life, edged it in so she would think it had crept up on her and taken place naturally. He made sure she didn't feel threatened by his feelings, or by the change in their relationship.

"Bloody hell."

She was suffering from information overload. What was needed was a coffee infusion before she gave this ridiculous notion any further thought. She headed for her favorite coffee shop in Coogee, resuming her thoughts once she was halfway through her extra large, double strength latte.

What was it Maggie had suggested? Daniel could be more of a victim than she was in this whole break up debacle. He might really love her.

Impossible.

Maybe not.

Now that she knew the truth about Leona and suspected the truth about her and Daniel's first incredible kiss, Maggie's idea didn't seem so ludicrous. What if Daniel did love her? What if he loved her from the start? She had to admit there was a miniscule possibility Daniel did love her and didn't know what to do about it. So he set her up. Made her fall in love with him. Slowly and sneakily.

First with Leona and then with...?

Well, she couldn't give him all the credit for what happened after the exhibition and then the next day in her flat. Hell, she was a willing participant in both of those...events.

What about the whole cricket bat incident?

What exactly was that business about Lexi attacking her own brother? Was it possible it had never happened? There were no bruises, no scratches, no real evidence to prove any assault actually took place.

Amy shook her head. Uh uh. Lexi *had* gone after him with a bat. It took a lot to piss Daniel off, and he was ticked that night. Furious with Lexi. But what if the incident hadn't been quite as bad as the siblings had made out? What if Daniel's injuries had not been quite so extensive—and he'd exaggerated a little?

The penny dropped and Amy's jaw almost hit the table for the second time that day.

Why the sneaky, devious, no-good, scheming sod. The devilish, sexy, irresistible, adorable sod. He'd tricked her. Found a neat little way to get her close to his almost-naked body. Given her the perfect excuse to touch him—over and over again—and she'd fallen for it.

Oh God. This meant Lexi was in on it too. She had to be. Had Daniel mobilized his troops to help him seduce her?

She took another sip of coffee and heard someone say, "Hello Amy."

Daniel's older sister stood by her table with her three-year-old son, Ben. Amy's heart went into overdrive. Christ. Was she in on Daniel's whole scheme as well? And if she was here, would Daniel be here too? Was she meeting him for a drink? Supper?

She realized how obtuse her thoughts were. Just because Sarah was here didn't necessarily mean Daniel was too. Even though she really, really, really wanted him to be here.

She smiled. "Hi yourself. I haven't seen you since Daniel's exhibition." The mere utterance of his name was enough to bring fresh pain slicing through her body.

"Yeah, I've been pretty busy. The kids take up all my time, but I wouldn't have it any other way." Sarah looked at Ben.

"Hello." He smiled at Amy, the creases in his cheeks reminding her of Daniel's sexy dimples.

"Hey Ben, what have you got there?"

"Thupper. Mummy'th giving uth a treat tonight. Fith and chipth."

Sarah shrugged. "It's one of those mad days. I just can't face cooking. With Daniel back today, the kids insisted we go see him as soon as he phoned. Time just vanished."

"Daniel got back today?" All at once Amy wanted to weep. Daniel was back home and he hadn't even phoned her.

Sarah hesitated before nodding and saying, "Yeah, a couple of hours ago."

"How is he?" She was desperate to hear anything about him.

Sarah looked uncomfortable. "He's okay, I guess. He said the shoot went well. All they have to do is polish a few things before the article is complete."

A steel band closed around her lungs, squeezing the air out. Daniel was back. "That's good." She was in abject misery and she prayed her face didn't reflect the inner turmoil churning inside her. "When will the article be published?" If she could just carry on making small talk for another few minutes, she could then make an excuse about having to leave. She would go home and throw herself on her bed and sob and sob and sob. Because Daniel was back and he hadn't phoned.

"I'm not sure," Sarah answered. "Why don't you ask him?"

The question caught her by surprise. "Uh, yeah...maybe I will." There was no chance of that happening.

"How have you been?" Amy thought she detected a note of concern in Sarah's voice.

"I'm fine," she lied.

"Ben, give me a minute please." Ben was tugging impatiently on Sarah's sleeve. She looked at Amy again. "You're looking...thinner."

Amy guessed it was not the word Sarah had wanted to use. Haggard, gaunt, drawn, miserable...any one of those would have been more suitable. "Uh, yes...I guess I've lost a bit of weight."

Sarah turned to her son and said distractedly, "Ben, can you please stop pulling me like that."

"But Mummy—"

"Honey, I'm talking to Amy now. Can you give me a minute?"

"But Mum? Mummy?"

Sarah cast a long-suffering glance at Amy and turned to

her son with a fond smile. "Yes, Ben. What is it?"

Ben stared wide-eyed at Amy. "Mummy, I don't think Amy hath a pig head."

"What?" Sarah's cheeks turned crimson.

"I don't think Amy hath a pig head," he lisped with all the innocence of a three-year-old.

"Ben! How can you say such a thing?" She shot Amy a desperate look.

"Well, Uncle Danny thaid he'd athk Amy to marry him if she'd thtop being pig-headed. But I don't think she hath a pig head."

ℂ

Operating on auto-pilot, Amy made it home. Somehow, she managed to finish her conversation with Sarah before stumbling home and collapsing into a chair in stunned disbelief.

Had she not been so astounded by Ben's comment, she would have thought it hilarious. As it was, Sarah almost crawled out of the shop in embarrassment. She cringed as she apologized for her son's tactlessness and then beat a hasty retreat before he could say any more.

Amy was left to figure out for herself what had preceded Ben's astounding disclosure and what she would do with all the information once she had it. A whirlwind of unanswered questions spun through her head.

Maggie thought Daniel might have genuine feelings for her. Leona was involved in a same sex relationship and was therefore not interested in him. Ben said Daniel wanted to marry her.

Immobile with disbelief, she allowed the facts to wash over her. Let the truth settle in. She took the extraordinary line-up of events in her life the last few months and finally saw them for what they really were.

The kisses, the sudden flare of desire, the irrepressible lust... None of it was coincidental. It was all part of his carefully masterminded plan to make his best friend fall in love with him, because he loved her.

What a brilliant strategy. It worked. Amy fell head-over-heels in love with him. Crazy, mad in love with him.

She just assumed he was incapable of loving her back.

Finally she understood what Maggie had been trying to tell her all along. Her fears about Daniel had been misplaced. Because of Simon and because of her father, she was afraid Daniel would betray her, leave her. She was terrified he wouldn't feel strongly enough about her to remain faithful. She didn't trust him. She had no faith in him. When he told her he loved her, she dismissed his emotions as the lustful yearnings of an adult man. When he spoke about wanting to be with her for always, she told him he was talking rubbish.

How wrong was she? She was way off the mark, mistaken, misguided. Her logic was flawed, faulty. How else could she put it? She fucked up.

If anything, she was the one who was disloyal to Daniel. Her lack of trust and faith in him were the ultimate betrayal. She should have known better. He was the single most honest person she knew. If he said he loved her, he loved her. Period. She should have accepted that as fact.

Instead she panicked. She was so threatened by the presence of another woman in Daniel's life that she ran away. Ran away from the best thing that had ever happened to her. From her best friend and lover and from her future.

All because she didn't have enough faith in Daniel to trust he wouldn't hurt her.

For hours she sat, motionless. Darkness approached. The last remaining patch of sunlight ebbed, shadowed and vanished. A dim glow was cast over the walls and chairs from the few streetlights twinkling outside. The near-complete blackness surrounding her reflected the emotion churning inside.

For hours she replayed the chain of events that brought her to her current situation until only two thoughts persistently echoed through her mind. All Daniel had ever given her was his love, and all she'd ever done in response was screw him over.

She failed him. Could he ever forgive her?

Chapter Fourteen

The thing about knowing someone loved you, Amy realized, was it was impossible to let go of the idea once it had taken root. He loved her. Daniel really loved her.

He hadn't planned on leaving her. He planned on marrying her. She'd put two and two together and got it wrong—horribly, hideously wrong. Before another minute of this god-awful misunderstanding passed she had to make it right.

Regardless of the fact it was well into the wee hours of the morning, she doused herself in Daniel's favorite perfume. The one that made him crazy, made him stand close and bury his nose in her neck. She searched for the black cocktail dress she wore the night of the exhibition, when things had taken such a steamy turn in their relationship. Impatience took hold of her when she couldn't find it and she threw on jeans and a tight T-shirt, too hurried to bother with a bra.

She grabbed her keys and ran. The desire to make things right with Daniel lent wings to her feet. Their relationship couldn't remain the same for one more second.

The ten minutes it took to drive to his unit and race to the front door seemed more like five hours. Amy pressed the buzzer, her heart pounding.

Open the door.

Blood roared in her ears as she buzzed again. *Where the*

hell is he?

She pressed a third time. Her hand shook. Her whole body shook.

Hurry up! Didn't he know they had to start the rest of their lives together? What was taking so long? She tapped her finger nervously against the doorpost. He was here. He *had* to be. According to Sarah, he'd returned home. Why wasn't he opening the door?

Finally, *finally*, came the sound of footsteps. She heard the metal creak of a lock turning and she wiped damp palms against her pants. Her breath came in short spurts and her cheeks burned.

The moment of reckoning had arrived.

The door opened and there he was. His face all warm and sleepy, his glorious curls, longer now and tousled. He wore a pair of boxers she guessed he must have pulled on in a hurry. They were inside out. She'd woken him. She didn't care. All she wanted was to throw herself in his arms and drown in his love.

"Amy?" He stared at her in disbelief. "What's going on? Is everything all right? Did someone die?" His voice sounded panicky.

"Everything's fine. There's something I need to tell you."

"At three in the morning?" He rubbed his eyes, forcing the sleep away.

"It couldn't wait." Her heart hammered.

He yawned and stretched at the same time, the movement pulling Amy's gaze down to the beautiful symmetry of his powerful chest.

"I'm sorry. I know it's late. I just didn't want to waste another minute." Adrenalin coursed through her veins. "Danny, I was wrong."

"You were?" He looked confused. Who could blame him? It was the middle of the night and he had no idea what she was doing here.

"Yes, I was. I was a fool. A blind, pig-headed fool. I can't believe it took me so—" Movement caught her eye.

Behind him a woman stood in his lounge. She wore a skimpy white nightgown, and looked remarkably like Janine Stillman.

"Daniel," Janine asked in a sleepy voice. "Is everything okay?"

If Daniel responded, Amy wasn't aware of it.

A bucket of cold, wet cement had been thrown at her, cutting off her air, blocking her senses, squelching her dreams. She couldn't breathe. Everything went dark.

No! Oh God, no.

Daniel was with another woman. Pain cut through her. Sensation drained from her body. She was rooted to the floor, paralyzed with shock. Time stood still.

Then instinct took over and she fled, ran for the safety of her car, desperate to put some distance between herself and them.

"You idiot! Idiot, idiot, idiot!" She cursed as she ran. How stupid was she? Why didn't she consider the fact Daniel might have company? Her stomach felt queasy. How did she get her facts so mixed up? Daniel was not in love with her.

"Idiot!" Hadn't she learned anything about men? They always moved on. Daniel especially. He was the king of moving on. Why should it be different with her? Because a three-year-old told her so?

The inky blackness of night obscured her vision and she stumbled over something on the footpath. Damn it, why weren't there any streetlights on? Tears sprang to her eyes. *Don't cry. Not yet. Wait until you get home.* Her hand shook violently as she tried to unlock her car but she couldn't seem to get the key in.

A hand clamped around her wrist from nowhere and she dropped her keys.

"Amy, damn it, wait!"

Daniel. He stood behind her, trapping her between the car and himself. *Oh God.* Her defenses were down. She was vulnerable. She couldn't face him like this.

"Leave me alone." She tried to pull her arm out of his grasp. Her efforts were futile.

"Calm down," he ordered.

Calm down? He was ordering her to calm down? She found him with another woman and *he* was ordering *her* to calm down? Rage replaced her shock.

"Let go!" She thrashed against him.

"Not until you tell me what you're doing here." His grip was a steel vise.

"I'm trying to go home!" she bellowed as she struggled to free herself. "But. You. Won't. Let me." With her free arm, she elbowed him in the ribs, hard.

"Shit!" He winced but still held tight. "That...hurt."

"Good." She lifted her arm to strike him again but before she could deliver another blow, he grabbed her other wrist and thrust himself forward, wedging her against the car. She couldn't move.

"Don't scream again," he warned. "You'll wake the neighbors."

She tried to wriggle her way out of his grasp, grinding her butt against him. He didn't budge, but his response was unmistakable. His erection grew and lodged between her buttocks. *Hypocrite.*

"Let. Me. Go."

"Quit struggling, will you?" He released her wrists and grabbed her hips, stilling her efforts.

Her body screamed in awareness. The last time they were this close they made love.

"Quit holding me prisoner."

"Just as soon as you tell me what the hell is going on. Why did you come?"

"It was a mistake," she tossed over her shoulder. "I shouldn't be here." Her body was stiff, poised and ready to bolt at the slightest hint of him weakening.

"Yeah, but you are and I want to know why. What were you trying to tell me?" His voice was low and his breath tickled her neck.

Every nerve ending stood to attention. "It's not important now."

"Five minutes ago it was important enough for you to wake me up in the middle of the night."

"Five minutes ago I didn't know you were with *her*." She immediately regretted her outburst. She'd let her guard down.

He spun her around. "Her?"

"Janine. Remember? The woman walking around half naked in your apartment?"

He dropped his hands and took a step back, muttering a few choice expletives. "You must pride yourself on your low opinion of me."

"You don't leave me much choice." She was hurting and she wanted to hurt him back. Hell, she wanted to punch his lights out.

212

"You see a woman in my apartment and automatically assume I'm sleeping with her?" He shook his head in disgust.

"What else am I supposed to think?" Her voice dripped with sarcasm. "That you're working on your article at three in the morning?"

"Something like that."

"'Something like that'? What's that supposed to mean?"

"It means she's staying at my place until we finish the article." He was shouting now. Well, not quite shouting, but his voice was much harsher than usual. "Is that such a crime?"

"It is if you're fucking her."

"Oh, and why is that? Because you're jealous?" This time when he spoke, his voice was soft and much, much colder.

She glared at him, unable to think of a snappy comeback. She was jealous. Christ, she was sick with jealousy.

"You lost your right to that emotion four weeks ago." His tone was icy.

The fight drained out of her and her shoulders sagged. What could she say? She didn't have the right to be jealous. "Look, I'm sorry I woke you. I shouldn't have come. Go back to Janine. I'm going home."

He swore again. "God, you're stubborn. You just don't get it, do you?"

She stared at him. "Get what?"

"I'm not sleeping with her."

Somewhere, a flicker of hope began to burn. "You're not?"

"No!"

"Why not?" She couldn't let it go altogether.

"*Ungh!* Why the hell do you think not?" He grabbed her shoulders and hauled her against him, forcing her face up to his. "Because I love *you*," he bit out before crushing his lips to hers.

Her world tipped off its axis and relief washed over her. He loved her. He held her so tight she couldn't breathe, but it didn't matter. He loved her. His mouth assaulted hers, bruising it, but she didn't care. He loved her.

He wrenched his lips from hers, his face inches from hers. "Wait...you still haven't told me what you're doing here."

Her voice was unsteady as she answered, breathless from the ferocity of his kiss. "I...came to...tell you I love you." It felt good to be back in his arms again. She was content to stay there for, oh, the rest of her life. "And to say I'm sorry for being such a fool and for not trusting you."

He stared at her. "Do you trust me now?" Although his arms tightened around her, his tone was unforgiving.

"With my life. And my heart."

"Why now? Why not weeks ago, when I told you how I felt?" The hurt she'd inflicted was evident in his voice. Her heart ached with remorse.

"I learned a few facts this morning that I never knew before." She took a deep breath. "They helped me understand our relationship a little better. All this time I've been scared to get involved with you. I was convinced you'd leave me and destroy our friendship in the process. I was so wrong. If anything, I hurt you. I didn't trust you or have enough faith to believe you would never jeopardize us."

Tears filled her eyes and spilled over. "When I told you we were finished, I was sure it was the right thing to do. Sure we'd be able to go back to being just friends. We'd done it before, after you...after the exhibition. I was sure we could do it again. I never stopped to consider you might not want to end our relationship. It never occurred to me you might honestly love me."

"Even when I told you I did?" His voice was raw.

"I didn't believe you. I was too busy protecting myself."

She looked up into his eyes. It was too dark to see them clearly, but she could feel his gaze on her face. A huge lump formed in her throat and she swallowed. "Danny, I love you. Please forgive me for hurting you. For betraying us. I was such an idiot."

"That you were."

"I want to make it right. I want so much more with you. Can we take our friendship to a new level? Please tell me you'll be my lover, my confidant, my partner. I want you. All of you." She repeated the words he said to her just a few weeks ago.

She raised her face to his and kissed him. A soft, gentle kiss, filled with the promise of everything she said. She loved him but still didn't know if he would forgive her.

He groaned against her lips and held her in an embrace so tender she almost wept again. "What took you so long, woman? I nearly gave up hope."

"Tell me you didn't. Tell me there's still hope for us."

"There's still hope for us. I love you, Morgan. If you give me the chance, I will never leave you. Ever."

"Is that a promise?"

"It's a vow."

"Oh God, Daniel, I'm so sorry I hurt you. Can you ever get past my appalling behavior?"

He pulled away slightly, and the flash of white teeth told her he grinned his devilish grin. "I'll consider it. If you accept you have to be punished for your actions."

A shiver of anticipation raced down her spine. "Punished?"

"Yes, you'll need to do penance." He kissed her. "It won't be easy." He worked his chest back and forth against her breasts. "It will involve a lot of time." Her nipples pebbled and she silently blessed her earlier haste that prevented her from putting on a bra.

"How much time?" Breath left her body as Daniel's hands crept under her shirt and cupped her bare flesh.

"Oh, a life sentence might cover it." He pushed her shirt up, leaned over and drew a nipple into his mouth.

"Hmm...that is a long time." Her back arched, allowing him easier access. She moaned as he sucked and sensation shot from her chest to between her legs, accentuating the urgent tug of arousal. "What do I have to do?"

He released her nipple and kissed her mouth again. "Marry me."

"You want me to marry you?" Her laugh was exultant.

"Yes."

"So Ben was right." She shook her head in amusement.

"Pardon?"

He must think her mad. He just asked her to marry him and she was talking about his nephew. "I saw Ben today."

Daniel looked baffled. "He told you I wanted to marry you?"

"Yes. And that you think I'm pig-headed."

"He said that?"

She waited as comprehension dawned on him. "Yeah, just before Sarah hightailed it out of the shop in embarrassment."

Daniel threw his head back and laughed. "Kids! I should haven known better than to say anything in front of him." He looked at her sheepishly. "I have a confession to make."

She would hear anything he had to say as long as he kissed

her first. Damn, she didn't want him to just kiss her, she wanted him to make love to her. Right here, right now. It had been a long, torturous four weeks. She needed to feel him inside her, to reinforce he really was hers, once and for all.

Need took precedence over everything right then and she leaned into him, hungrily taking his mouth in a very long kiss. "You've done something you shouldn't have?" Slightly breathless, she ran her hand over his boxers and cupped his stiff penis. God, she'd forgotten how amazing it felt to touch him.

"Morgan, oh, Christ...wait..." he said in a strangled whisper and stepped backwards, pulling out of her grasp. Amy almost cried out in frustration, but Daniel's fingers closed around her wrist. "C'mon," he growled and was already moving, tugging her along with him.

She stumbled after him as he half ran, half marched her around the side of the building. The thirty seconds it took to lead her to an isolated nook, hidden from possible car headlights, stretched out like an eternity. But then he was pushing her against the wall, kissing her again, and her hand was inside his boxers, palming his erection and everything was right with the world. Everything was more than right. It was un-bloody-believable. She was back in Daniel's arms, where she belonged.

The moan that followed could have come from either of them, she wasn't sure.

She drew her mouth away from his. "Your confession?" she prompted, and would have said more but was incapable of coherent speech.

He nodded, breathed and nodded again. "I, um...kind of made something up."

"You did?" She pumped his shaft, then bit her cheek as a

wave of desire crashed over her.

He struggled to speak. "Know how, um...Leona was...interested in me?" His breathing shallowed. "Well...that might have been a...bit of an...exaggeration."

"How so?" She enjoyed letting him suffer a little, knowing she was ethically bound by her profession and could never tell Daniel she already knew all this. The rough skin of his unshaven jaw prickled her lips as she trailed kisses along it.

"She's not interested in me." It was his turn to torment her and he did so ever so effectively, running a hand over her pants and pressing gently against her clit.

"She's not?" She sucked her lip and tightened her grip, her urgency for him increasing a hundredfold.

"No. She's gay. She has a girlfriend."

"You lied?" She pretended to be horrified, but all she could really think about was his hand. She rotated her pelvis as his fingers massaged her through her jeans.

"I may have stretched the truth a little."

It was difficult to concentrate. His tongue did crazy things to her neck. She pumped his dick a little faster and was rewarded with a low groan in her ear.

"Cricket-bat incident?" she asked. Again, full sentences were beyond her.

"Uh, I may have stretched the truth on that one too," he rasped.

"I figured." She smiled and squirmed as he nibbled her jaw.

"It was all justified," he assured her. "I had to present you with motivating grounds to kiss me. To touch me." He caught her lips with his and her mouth parted instantly. He needed no motivating grounds now.

When he pulled away, leaving her gasping for more, he

said, "I knew that if we could just get past that first kiss, if I could just get you excited to touch me, I could convince you to love me, slowly and surely."

"It worked." She needed to show him how much. Now. "I do love you."

"I love you too."

"Prove it."

Daniel did not disappoint. In less than a second he was making short work of her jeans and panties. She took the opportunity to shove his boxers down over his hips.

"God, Morgan, I missed you." He dipped his hand between her legs and her moisture oozed onto his fingers.

She was so ready for him. She clasped his erection and pulled him closer. Later, there would be time for slow and sensual lovemaking, kisses and snuggles, foreplay and after play. There would be a lifetime for it. Right now she just needed him to make love to her. Needed him to affirm she was his. Always.

She wound her arms around his broad shoulders, relishing the hard, male muscle in his chest and back, and pressed her hips up into his. "Show me."

He did. Right there against the wall. While she slipped first one leg and then the other around his waist, he hoisted her up by placing two firm hands beneath her butt. Then, with a low groan, he plunged into her, filling her, completing her.

It was a wild, hot, desperate ride. Their frenetic pace matched her feverish need for him and she came quickly, high on the knowledge that he loved her.

When she'd milked the last drop of semen from his body, he held her in his arms, and whispered, "Welcome home, my love."

Several moments passed before Amy felt capable of either movement or conversation. Daniel slipped out of her when she lowered her legs to the ground, but he did not release her.

Her heart still pounded unevenly in her chest. "You made up the whole Leona story just so I'd fall for you?" Although she already knew the truth, she was still wonder-struck.

"I had to. I couldn't let our friendship go on any longer without letting you know how I felt, but I couldn't risk telling you before I was sure you felt the same. I knew you'd doubt my motives." He frowned and his hands stilled. "I was right."

She hugged him tight. "I was wrong. I'm sorry. Being in love with you is all so new, so uncertain. I didn't know how to deal with it. I was so sure I'd just be another in a long line of girlfriends."

He shook his head and looked at her, disbelieving. "You still don't get it, do you?"

"Get what?"

"I've always loved you."

"Huh?" *What?*

"For as long as I can remember. I fell in love with you the day we met at school. Why do you suppose I've never been able to commit to another woman?"

He had a reason? "Why?"

"Because she wasn't you. None of them were. They could never measure up. Hard as I tried with some of them, I'd always end up wanting you."

"Me? It's been me all along?" Her heart was just about to burst.

"Morgan, it's only ever been you."

She couldn't hold back her grin. It pretty much exploded onto her face. "Then I guess I'll just have to accept your punishment."

"You'll marry me?" She could hear the smile in his voice.

"On one condition."

"Name it."

"Promise it's forever."

"Amy, my friend, I promise. Trust me when I say all I've ever wanted is forever with you."

This time, Amy trusted him.

About the Author

To learn more about Jess Dee please visit www.jessdee.com. Send an email to jess@jessdee.comor stop. Stop by her blog and say hello: http://jessdee.wordpress.com/.

Can one wild night of passion turn into the romance of a lifetime?

Ask Adam
© 2007 Jess Dee

Lexi Tanner's got a major problem: AJ Riley, the man she's about to approach for a hefty donation, turns out to be the stranger she shared a night of steamy sex with less than a week past. She'll do anything to raise money for a children's charity—anything except sell herself. Now how can she ask AJ for money without it seeming like he's paying for sexual favors?

If there's one thing the past has taught Adam "AJ" Riley, it's that loving someone can only lead to pain. He knows he shouldn't feel so attracted to Lexi, and he definitely shouldn't trust a woman who'd sleep with a man one week and approach him for money the next. Yet somehow Lexi breaks through all his barriers. His instincts tell him to run but his heart wants to give Lexi—and love—a second chance. How can he let go of his tragic past and still protect his battered heart?

Warning, this title contains the following: steamy sex, graphic language and red-hot romance.

Available now in ebook and print from Samhain Publishing.

Printed in the United States
143475LV00003B/8/P